The Vienna Trilogy

BOOK THREE

Stopping the Russian Bear

by Tom Gilligan

Illustrations by Everett Walker

Intelligence e-Publishing Company
Cape Cod, Massachusetts

IEP

Intelligence Book Division

Intelligence e-Publishing Company, Cape Cod, Massachusetts

Illustrations by Everett Walker.

Book Design by Charles King (ckmm.com).

Cover image courtesy of Magnus Johansson.

ISBN 978-0-9729659-5-8

Library of Congress Control Number: 2022917921

Contents

Prologue

As junior spy David Hale became actively involved in the Cold War in 1947, he had no way of knowing just how pivotal Austria—and especially its capital city, Vienna—was becoming in the upcoming struggle between East and West. To the east of Austria, everything in Europe had already fallen under the brutal Russian Communist control of the Red Army and the Soviet Secret Police. To Austria's west, every European nation was struggling to retain its freedom and independence.

Out in faraway Asia, the Chinese Communist Army—with Soviet Russian support and encouragement—was on the brink of conquering all of mainland China, which it would accomplish by 1949.

Eleven-year-old David Hale, barely two years after World War II, had joined an important struggle for freedom at a dangerous time and place. Vienna, Austria—and David himself—were at the forefront of the upcoming global battle that would be fought—not by armies dropping bombs and a world in a fighting "hot" war—but rather, by diplomats and secret spies who would engage in a different kind of contest—a "cold" war that would last almost 50 years.

Dedication

To the people of Ukraine
valiantly fighting for freedom and independence
against the criminal invasion
of the brutal Russians
whose military and Secret Police
have produced an uninterrupted
and sordid history
dating back to the Russian Revolution.

Glory to Ukraine! Glory to Heroes!

Post-War Chaos across Europe

1

Post-War Chaos

The Date: Monday, July 7, 1947
Downtown Vienna, Austria

Even though the Hales had managed to rid themselves of the
Nazi trio, there was still some urgent work that needed to be
done to support the Intelligence Group. The following morning, a Monday, David Hale, his father, and Thor headed for
downtown Vienna. *Living conditions** were far from normal and
the city was still a mess from all the wartime bombing. The
Austrian *capital city*† itself was being run by the military *authorities*‡ of four different countries: the United States, England,
France, and Russia. To make things even more difficult, one of
these four *occupying*§ countries was making things worse. The
Russians, rather than helping Austria recover from the war,
were doing their best to see that Austria would never be an
autonomous¶ or free country again. So far, the Americans and
British had been able to prevent the Russians, who had already

---

*   Living Conditions: The kinds and quality of buildings, homes, trains,
     food supply, and health care.
†   Capital City: Most important city in a state or country where the gov-
     ernment has its main offices.
‡   Authorities: Top or most important leaders or officials.
§   Occupying: Living in a country.
¶   Autonomous: Ruling your own country and making your own rules
     and laws.

conquered the countries east of Austria and Germany, from pushing any further across Western Europe.

As things turned out, however, America would need to be both patient and strong over several decades to solve the 'Soviet Russia Problem.' It would take the next eight years—until 1955—before the Red Army was *pressured** enough to leave Vienna and the rest of Austria. It would require another 35 years—until 1990—before the Russian-led Empire known as the Soviet Union or *USSR*,† would itself *collapse*.‡ Only then would the countries and the people of Eastern Europe have a chance to be *genuinely*§ free.

The victories in the years ahead by the *Western Powers*⁋ over Communist Russia were made possible *primarily*** because of both the strong United States and British Military Forces in Europe, as well as the good work of the U.S. Embassies—their diplomats and their secret spies—operating in key cities such as Vienna, Berlin, Warsaw, and Moscow. It was in Vienna where young David Hale had recently joined the battle on the side of freedom-loving people everywhere. He was at the right place—Vienna, Austria—at the right time—1947. And, as it would turn out, he was just the right kid for the secret and dangerous work that lay ahead.

---

*   Pressured: Being tough with the Russians and not letting them have their way.

†   USSR: Union of Soviet Socialist Republics included Russia and all the countries in Eastern Europe that had been conquered by the Red Army and the Communist political leaders in Moscow.

‡   Collapse: Fall apart or come crashing down.

§   Genuinely: Really or truly.

⁋   Western Powers: Led by the United State of America, included England, France, Canada, Italy, and the nations of Scandinavia.

**   Primarily: Mainly, principally, and mostly.

His father—medical doctor and senior spy Matt Hale—was mighty proud of what David had done so far. After all, it was the boy's *superb** slingshot skill that had made it possible for Dr. Hale to safely contact the Polish scientist, Dr. Kaminski, and rescue him from the Russian zone up in Linz, Austria. In addition, it was David and his German Shepherd Thor who had found the gold, counterfeit money, and the false travel documents that had been hidden late in the war to help important Nazi war criminals escape to South America. The Hale team of boy and dog also found a secret Nazi treasure map in the lining of one of the trunks and that would become quite important to the Americans for learning where the Gestapo had hidden Chief Himmler's stolen art.

Now, father and son were in downtown Vienna in support of another intelligence operation—this one designed to give the Americans a secret agent in Warsaw, the important capital of Poland, which both the German and the Russian Red Army had attacked in 1939. Warsaw lies 350 miles to the east of Vienna and about a third of the way to Moscow, Russia's capital city.

In Poland, as well as in the dozen other *unfortunate*† Eastern European nations that remained occupied by the Red Army after World War II, the Russian Secret Police had begun to tighten their *chokehold*‡ on the local government and on the citizens. The Russians *essentially*§ followed the same program

---

* Superb: Wonderful, excellent unusually good.
† Unfortunate: Unlucky.
‡ Chokehold: Complete control as when a wrestler places his hands around the other guy's throat.
§ Essentially: In most important ways.

that the German Nazis had *imposed** early in the war—after all, Nazis and Communists in fact are similar when it comes to limiting freedom. Each of their *systems*† requires their leaders to have total control over its citizens, who are important only as long as they support the goals and programs of the government. This horrible way of thinking explains why Nazis and Communists murdered and imprisoned so many millions of their own people. It is also why so many of their own citizens tried every possible way to escape to *The West.*‡

As father and son settled into their *lodging*,§ they did not at first discuss the larger problems facing Europe or Austria. They had to get busy—they had work to do. They reviewed their day's tasks and discussed what they needed to accomplish over the next few days. To begin with, Matt Hale had to go over to the conference center where the international medical meetings were scheduled to begin the next morning. He had to find the location of the Polish Officer in charge of security for the visiting Polish *delegation.*¶ His name: Major Piotr Gorski—he was the American Embassy's *recruitment target.*** (During the German occupation, Gorski had used his middle name, Otto, but that was too Germanic for him to use once the Russians took over Poland.)

Matt Hale's first job was to find a way for his U.S. Embassy friend, Visitor, to meet Major Gorski—alone and safely. Visitor

---

*   Imposed: To force on a person, group of people or nation.
†   Systems: The kinds of government they had.
‡   The West: The countries of Western Europe, America and nations living in freedom.
§   Lodging: The place where a person is staying, in this case a hotel.
¶   Delegation: The group attending the conference from the same country, in this case Poland.
** Recruitment Target: A person whom an intelligence service wants to recruit as a spy.

spoke *fluent** Polish which he had learned as a child from his parents when they moved from Poland to the U.S. in the 1920s.

The American Intelligence Group was fairly confident from what they had been told by an earlier Polish *defector†* that Major Gorski was likely recruitable. First, however, the Americans needed to meet and speak privately with Gorski. The American goal in this operation was not to get the Major to defect and go to the United States. Instead, the American plan was to recruit and train him right there in Vienna—starting this week if possible. If the recruitment and spy training went well, Gorski would return from Vienna to his security position back in Poland. From then on, he would be operating as a secret spy for the Americans.

What made this operation more difficult and dangerous was the risk it involved. If the Russians in *Warsaw‡* were to catch Gorski spying for the Americans and reporting secretly to them, either now or in the future, they would do what they always do when they catch such a spy—they would torture and shoot him.

Recalling the rescue operation of the Polish scientist—Dr. Kaminski—David was thinking that the Mercedes twin, with its secret hiding place, would be used to sneak Major Gorski out of Vienna. So, he asked his dad whether he would have to do the egg *diversion trick§* all over again. He *assured¶* his dad that he was ready to do it again if that was what was needed.

---

* Fluent: Speaking and understanding a foreign language very well.
† Defector: One who runs away from his country and helps his country's enemies.
‡ Warsaw: Capital city of Poland at the time under control of the Red Army.
§ Diversion Trick: A way of fooling the Russian guard.
¶ Assured: Promised or guaranteed.

Matt Hale smiled and said, "Not at all, Son, but thanks. No eggs—this time, we do not plan to use the twin car but, instead, want this fellow to return to Poland and from then on report to us secretly. But, that would be true only if he looks like he could be a good spy—and not get caught by the Russians. If he can do all that, his secret reporting could keep us *informed** on what the Russian Red Army and Secret Police are doing. Being so informed, in turn, will help us make sure the Russians are not successful in their program to conquer all of Western Europe. Unfortunately, most of Eastern Europe is already under the control of the Red Army and Russian Secret Police."

Dr. Hale went on, "America needs spies reporting to us in Warsaw, the Polish capital, more than we need another Polish refugee going on to live in the United States. Keep in mind son, if America and England had recruited and trained spies inside Germany back in the 1930s—before World War II—we might very well have dealt with Hitler and the Nazi *madness*† earlier. Who knows, we might have been able to avoid World War II altogether. Just think of how many millions of innocent lives would have been saved if America—*before the war*—had good reporting spies in Germany, in Japan, or both."

David listened intently to his father's words and was beginning to understand the *big picture*.‡ The West, led by America and England, had only recently decided to be part of a *joint program*§ to contain the Russians and keep them from conquering other lands and countries. That program and *policy*¶ to defend

---

*   Informed: Knowing or fully advised.
†   Madness: Insane, as Adolph Hitler clearly was.
‡   Big Picture: The background and broad understanding of what was going on all across Europe as well as in Austria.
§   Joint Program: Something done as partners working together.
¶   Policy: The decisions and goals of a country in dealing with other nations.

Western Europe, in fact, came to be known as *Containment.** By 1947, when the Hales joined the fight on the side of freedom, the Russians in Eastern Europe had already conquered much territory, including Albania, Armenia, Byelorussia, Bulgaria, Czechoslovakia, Estonia, Georgia, Hungary, Latvia, Lithuania, Romania, Ukraine and the eastern regions of Germany and Austria. In addition, Russia controlled the nations of Uzbekistan, Azerbaijan, Kazakhstan, Kyrgyzstan, Tajikistan and Turkmenistan. Communists were in control of Yugoslavia and Chinese Communists would soon win the civil war in China. Meanwhile, local Communists were gaining strength in France and Italy and were becoming more powerful in Greece as well as Turkey. So, anyone looking at the map of the world in mid-1947 would surely conclude that Communists were taking control of much of the world.

To succeed in stopping the Russians from making even more gains, therefore, the Western Powers needed intelligence reporting from spies in the right places. The week's attempted recruitment operation of Major Gorski in Vienna—if success-ful—could help do just that, because Poland borders Germany, Soviet Russia, Byelorussia, Lithuania, Czechoslovakia, and Ukraine.

The Hales were spending the week in *temporary quarters*[†] behind the Rothschild "Displaced Persons" (DP's)[‡] Hospital.

---

*   Containment: The name for the policy or game plan of America, England and the Western Powers for dealing with the Russian Communists and the Red Army—not letting them conquer Western Europe.

†   Temporary Quarters: Housing for a short period of time.

‡   Displaced Persons (DP's): These were the millions of refugees who had lost everything in the war and wandered around the continent for weeks, months, or years until they were able to find a new home— assuming they were able to escape the Russians who kidnapped many hundreds of thousands to work in their prisons, factories, and mines.

This *clinic** since the war ended had been taking care of refugees who could not return to their native lands all across
Eastern Europe. It had been a little over two years since the
Russian Army *stormed*[†] into Austria, capturing Vienna before
going on to capture the Nazi capital of Berlin. All across Europe
when WWII ended in May 1945, 16 million refugees were left
scattered hundreds and in some cases thousands of miles from
the towns and villages where they had lived before the war.
During 1945 and 1946, train-loads, bus-loads and wagon-loads
of displaced refugees were sent back to their homelands—many
not *voluntarily*.[‡] In fact, hundreds of thousands of them were
sent back forcibly, especially to Soviet Russia.

The Eastern European refugees in Austria who knew too
well the horror of Communism—and what living under the
brutal Russians would mean to them and their families—had
no desire whatsoever to go back to their *pre-war*[§] homes. For
people living in normal times and places, returning to their
homeland is usually welcomed as a great blessing. For those
forcibly sent to Poland and other Eastern European nations in
the grip of the Russians Secret Police, going back home was a
horrible curse. Many thousands of refugees instead chose to
commit suicide.[¶]

Dr. Matt Hale, in his medical work since arriving in Austria,
was deeply involved in giving *humanitarian*[**] support to these

---

*   Clinic: A small hospital.
†   Stormed: Violently attacked or invaded.
‡   Voluntarily: By free choice and decision.
§   Pre-War: Before the war, back in the 1930s.
¶   Commit Suicide: To kill oneself.
** Humanitarian: Caring for and helping people who are poor, helpless
    and sick.

poor, displaced peoples. He treated and cured infectious diseases affecting a high *percentage** of the refugee population—most of whom had not received medical or dental care for the whole period of the war. Rather than helping them, however, the Russians were instead stealing food from Austrian farms. *As a result, over half of the hospital patients in Vienna in 1946 and 1947*—foreign refugees as well as Austrians—were suffering from extreme *malnutrition.†* A good part of the population was on the verge of starving to death.

When he was not doing medical work and wearing his doctor's *garb,‡* senior spy Matt Hale was fighting another deadly infection of sorts—that of the *murderous§* Russian Secret Police. These evil *brutes⁋* used kidnappings, terror campaigns and even murders to try to conquer The West. In 1945 and 1946 alone, the Russians kidnapped around 130,000 refugees and sent them from Austria to *slave camps*** as far away as the frozen region of Siberia, in northern Russia.

Among the permanent refugees who escaped from Eastern Europe and Russia was a sizeable group of displaced persons who no longer had a homeland—they had nowhere really to go. In the early 1940's, the German Army had destroyed their homes and villages, stole their belongings and killed most

---

* Percentage: A share of something such as a quarter, a half or all; usually written 25%, 50% or 100%.

† Malnutrition: Starvation.

‡ Garb: Clothing or dress.

§ Murderous: People who kill many people, usually those who are completely innocent of doing anything wrong.

⁋ Brutes: People who behave like wild animals.

** Slave Camps: The Communist Government sent prisoners to camps in the far north and worked them to death cutting trees and mining.

of their families. The German Army, and especially the SS/ Gestapo, did this in every country they invaded. In Austria alone, the Nazis sent around 65,000 Austrian Jews to death camps between 1938 and 1945.

When the war was over, the Russians did not want this group of refugees back. The Jewish people of Europe found at war's end that they had no safe place to go. They had been robbed entirely of their European *roots.** They knew that their former *countrymen*† across Europe would not let them return to their lifelong homes.

As a result, homeless Jews stuck after the war in Austria— even more so in Germany itself—were trying to find a way to depart for England, Canada, Australia, and the United States—to any country where they might be able to rebuild their lives in freedom. Many Jews went southward through Italy and then to the *Middle East*‡ where they would build the Jewish State of Israel. Yes, the Jewish people of Europe who had suffered millions of dead under the Nazis had to get away from the European *continent*§ altogether when the war was over. *Ironically,*§ escaping Jewish refugees would in many cases end up taking the same escape routes used by *fleeing*** German war criminals.

---

* Roots: Backgrounds and the countries or towns where people come from.
† Countrymen: People who come from the same town, city or country.
‡ Middle East: The lands south and east of The Mediterranean Sea.
§ Continent: A division of the world by map-making geographers into seven major land masses: Asia, Europe, Africa, North America, South America, Australia and Antarctica.
§ Ironically: The opposite of what is ordinarily expected.
** Fleeing: Those running away .

When Matt Hale explained all of this to David that evening over dinner, the boy was even more pleased that his dad and he had stopped SS Colonel Schmidt and his two goons from making a *clean getaway*.* Later, as he lay his head on the pillow, the boy looked up at the Vienna sky and whispered, "Good night, Anne. Good night Margot."

It had been barely five years since the Frank family first had gone into hiding in Amsterdam, Holland. David Hale, for his part, was becoming increasingly aware that there was a lot more work that had to be done—work for spies—work for him. In the face of such evil, he wasn't all that sure that there is a Heaven and a Hell when our life is over. His mom said yes; his dad said he did not know—but he certainly hoped so. David Hale was quickly learning that there certainly can be a *Hell on Earth*† for innocent people who fall victim to the Nazis or the Communists—as far as David Hale was concerned, from everything his dad had shared, the two powers were *identical*.‡

---

*   Clean getaway: Escaping with no problems of any kind.
†   Hell on Earth: What life is like when so many bad, evil things are happening and life is filled with misery and suffering.
‡   Identical: Exactly the same.

David Approaches Red Storm Hotel

2

*Casing** The Target Hotel

The Date: July 8, 1947
Early Tuesday Morning.

David woke up earlier than usual. The morning sounds of downtown Vienna were different for him than the Hale castle sounds which at dawn included roosters crowing down at the Vogel cottage. Across the castle, each morning David could hear birds chirping high from the parapet while they surveyed the countryside for hawks and other *predators*.[†] Now, awakened by the unfamiliar sounds of the city, the new junior spy was up and out exploring at a time well before the medical conference visitors staying at the nearby hotels. Most of these visitors had spent the previous evening drinking Russia's and Poland's favorite alcoholic drink, *vodka*.[‡] With almost no one out in the streets this early in the day, the boy and dog strolled around the downtown area without ever seeing a single Russian.

David decided, therefore, to take a look at the Red Storm Hotel, where his dad said the Polish delegation was staying. It was within walking distance of the center of the city and just inside the Russian sector. Using the map, David had no

---

*   Casing: Very careful collection of information about a place of interest in an intelligence operation.
†   Predators: Animals hunting and hoping to eat them.
‡   Vodka: A clear white alcoholic drink made from potatoes.

trouble finding the Red Storm Hotel. He took a deep breath and approached the front door, but stopped for a few seconds to look back at Thor. He told his *sidekick** to sit outside while he went in. David had no idea what to expect.

His dad, meanwhile, had gotten off to an even earlier start that morning and had been gone when David awoke. Dr. Hale was at the nearby Rothschild Refugee Hospital which had some new patients who had arrived there in terrible condition. Most had either typhus or typhoid fever. To make matters even worse, the patients were suffering from *starvation*.† Dr. Hale made his *rounds*‡ and had to put aside his thoughts of Russians, Poles and spies for the time being. For the next two hours, he simply was Dr. Hale and the *desperate*§ hospital patients were glad to have him there. When he left the hospital later as the sun was rising, he *converted*⁋ back to senior intelligence officer, intent on tracking down Polish Major Gorski for the U.S. Embassy. But, he first had to get back to his hotel and prepare for the rest of the day ahead.

Just a few blocks away, David was walking in the door of the Polish delegates' hotel where he met an elderly man working at the Red Storm Hotel's front desk and who greeted him in German, "Good morning, can I help you, young man? You are out so early."

At this point David decided to answer him in German since

---

*   Sidekick: From the world of the American West that David loved so much, it means a cowboy's partner.
†   Starvation: Poor diet; not enough food to eat; hunger; malnutrition.
‡   Rounds: The visits to sick patients a doctor makes to see how patients are feeling.
§   Desperate: Just about without hope.
⁋   Converted: Changed into or became again.

he had been practicing with Frau Vogel. He replied, "No, I am waiting to see my father downtown. I came in here hoping to get a drink of water." The old man said he would get it for him and be right back.

It was then that David spotted two big, rough-looking men sitting in chairs in a far corner of the *front lobby**. They were guards who looked like they had been up all night. Their clothes were wrinkled and they were unshaven. They were clearly carrying guns as David could tell by the big bulges in their brown overcoats. He knew they were Russian guards, for he had heard enough Russians speaking at the different checkpoints around Vienna and Linz when out with his dad.

The junior spy sat down on an old sofa that looked like it had been through two wars. Its covering was badly worn and *dingy†* as was the carpeting on the floor. There was an old iron lamp in the corner. In front of the sofa was a small wooden table on which David spotted two stacks of papers. One stack had a map of downtown Vienna that showed the Conference Center as well as the nearby hotels and restaurants. The other pile of papers displayed an hourly conference schedule for the entire week. *Specifically,‡* it was the program for the Polish delegates who were in town attending the medical meetings.

David *assumed§* his dad would want to look at both papers, so he moved himself slowly over on the sofa to be within arm's reach of both stacks. The two Russians across the lobby paid no

---

* Front lobby: The entrance way of a hotel where guests wait for visitors.

† Dingy: Dirty.

‡ Specifically: Exactly.

§ Assumed: Thought or believed in advance.

attention to him. After all, their orders for the week did not say anything about being on the lookout for kids. The guards were there to prevent any of the Polish delegates from defecting to The West, period. If anyone did defect, then the guards might as well run away too because they would be in a lot of trouble if they returned to Poland without all of the delegates. Looking at the stacks of paper for a moment, David thought how his dad might act in this situation; he decided to move slowly and stay cool. No, he would not rush things. First, he would try to figure out what was going on. He wanted to see how alert the two Russians really were. And it did not take long for David to realize that they had no interest in him or in the stacks of paper.

Rather, their attention and eyes were on a cleaning girl who was mopping up the lobby. They kept trying to strike up a conversation with her but had no luck. After all the *assaults**
on Austrian women by Russian soldiers in the months after the Battle of Vienna, like most Austrian women she had no interest at all even talking to them.

Knowing the guards were distracted, the junior spy made his move. David *casually*† reached out and took one paper from each pile of papers and brought them down to the floor. He then reached down as if he was going to tie his shoes but, instead, quickly folded the papers he had swiped and slid them into his socks. David then reached for the glass of water, took a quick sip, slowly got up and walked to the front desk. He thanked the old gentleman behind the front desk for the drink and then headed out the door.

---

*   Assaults: Physical attacks.
†   Casually: In a slow, natural way that did not draw attention.

Thor stood waiting outside the hotel doing exactly as he had been told. David's heart was beating a little faster than usual but, when he got out on the street and away from the big Russian guards, he quickly relaxed and felt satisfied. Boy and dog then headed back to their hotel. Matt Hale had arrived there some minutes before and was wondering where they had been. "How was your walk, Son? See anything interesting?" The doctor was seated in the lobby which was as clean as a hospital *operating room** compared to the *rundown*† place where the Polish delegates were staying.

The junior spy, before answering, looked around to make sure no one else could hear their conversation. David was sitting across from his dad and this time it was he who asked a question. "Can you guess what I found down at the hotel where the Poles are staying? Two guesses, Dad, go ahead."

Now the dad was at a loss for words as he tried to figure out what made David so *spunky*‡ so early in the day. "Okay, son. Before we get to the Red Storm Hotel, I am guessing you found a German Luger below the castle parapet. Herr Vogel said he had seen it but later it was gone. You probably hid it in your closet flooring is my guess. How am I doing, Son? Okay so far?"

Now it was David who was *on the spot*§—he had planned to show the Nazi Colonel's pistol to his dad, but wanted to hold onto it a day or two just for the excitement of finally having a

---

* Operating room: A special room where they do surgery and must be perfectly clean to avoid infection.

† Rundown: A place that is worn out from years of use and years without getting fixed, painted, or repaired.

‡ Spunky: In a happy mood.

§ On the spot: In a difficult position or in some trouble.

Luger—hopefully one of his own, that is, if his dad would let him keep it.

But, the senior spy admitted he had no idea what David had found downtown this morning and said so. "David, I don't have a clue what you may have found at the other hotel. Tell me and I will show you how to use and handle the Luger safely—once we get some free time back at the castle. Lugers, after all, are not toys, which I am sure you know very well. So tell me, what did you find this morning that might be so interesting? I have to get going and figure out how, when and where I can get our friend Visitor in contact with the Polish fellow he is after."

'Well, Dad, maybe I have saved you some time!" Reaching down inside his socks, the junior spy pulled out the two papers, unfolded and placed them on the table in front of his dad. "What do you think, Dad? These were just sitting on a table in the lobby at the Red Storm Hotel. They were placed there for the conference delegates most likely by two lazy Russian guards more interested in a young Austrian cleaning girl than in doing their jobs. Looks like they are written in Russian and Polish, which you can read—which you, dad, can understand."

"This is good, but how could you be so sure they would not see—or worse—catch you taking their papers, Son? What made you think it could be done so safely?"

"I am telling you, Dad, I studied the two guards carefully and figured I could have taken their boot laces *unnoticed*.* In the fifteen minutes or so I was in the lobby, these guards never once looked my way—never looked at me—probably would

---

* Unnoticed: Not having been seen.

not remember I was even there. The two stacks of paper had many copies. I just took one from each stack. As you saw, I had them in my socks. And when I walked towards the door to leave the Red Storm Hotel, the guards were still trying to chat with this Austrian girl who seemed to ignore them the entire time." Matt Hale *skimmed** the papers, smiling and said, "David, you just saved me a half and maybe an entire day of work. Good for you. Now, get something to eat. As for Thor's meal, you will find it is up in our room.

"And two things: Yes, the Luger will be yours some day when I am sure you can handle it safely. The pistol would be perfect for tunnel rats when you are a bit older. But for now, I removed the firing pin so the gun cannot be fired and no one can get hurt. Also, next time, you can take those guards' boot laces, too! You, Son, are getting pretty darn good for a beginner—no, *very good!*"

David tried not to *gloat,*† but was smiling widely as he and Thor started up the stairs to their room.

---

*   Skimmed: Read quickly.
†   Gloat: To brag or try to show off.

Visitor Contacts the Hales

3

*Ops Planning** with Visitor

Visitor arrived at the hotel room a little later, just as David was taking Thor out for another walk. He greeted the boy, as always, with a warm smile and then proceeded to give Thor a neck and back rub. He knew all about the dog's war record and had a very special fondness for this particular patrol dog. Visitor too had served in combat early in the war, before he was moved into Army Intelligence when it was found that he had spoken Polish since childhood. As far as learning a foreign language goes, Polish is one of the most difficult to learn—more so than Russian or German, neither of which languages is all that easy.

Once David and Thor headed out the door, the two senior spies—Matt Hale and Visitor—*got down to business.*† Matt Hale had spread a map of downtown Vienna on the table and was reading through the information sheets David had brought back from the Red Storm Hotel. Visitor was delighted to learn that David had picked up the papers that could help them *isolate*‡ Major Gorski. This would help Visitor find a time in the conference schedule when he could contact and be alone with Gorski for a few hours. Visitor would need time to *determine*§

---

*   Ops Planning: An abbreviation for Operations Planning which is the careful preparation for an intelligence action.
†   Got Down to Business: Started working.
‡   Isolate: Get him alone.
§   Determine: Figure out.

whether this Polish Officer was *recruitable** as believed and reported by the earlier Polish defector, Dr. Kaminski. Visitor was fairly confident that, if he could meet with Gorski privately for a few hours, he would be able to *assess*† him and see if he really was the type of man who could live with the risks of spying under the watchful eyes of the Russians. He might well be such a rare individual. After all, he had managed to survive since the war ended without the Communists ever realizing he was not happy with them and their system of government.

Spying inside the *enemy camp*‡—for example, back in Poland—is far more difficult than just trying to survive there. It requires an exceptional kind of courage which even those who are bravely fighting in combat may not possess. In combat, things happen fast and soldiers have *buddies*§ fighting alongside of them. War fighters also have the extra boost that comes from their own adrenalin. In spying, by contrast, one is usually alone among enemies, things can move slowly over a long period of time, and there are no buddies around to help deal with the risks and dangers from the Secret Police. Furthermore, a spy's own adrenalin could become his own worst enemy. For, if he got too nervous, the Russians might wonder why Major Gorski suddenly seemed so *agitated*.¶ Spies who are able to survive in

---

*   Recruitable: Able to be recruited because he is unhappy with the Soviet system.

†   Assess: Come to understand all about a person to decide if he can do a certain job, in this case spying.

‡   Enemy Camp: Inside Poland or Russia where the Russian Secret Police control security, telephones, cameras, listening devices and the very life of the citizens.

§   Buddies: Friends and pals, fellow soldiers.

¶   Agitated: Nervous and shaky.

the enemy camp need to possess three C's—they have to be "cool, calm and *collected*."*

Finally, the stress on a spy is made even greater because the Russian Secret Police make sure that everyone knows what happens to enemy spies whom they catch operating *on their turf*.[†] They kill them most certainly but, first, they *torture*[‡] them in order to learn as much as possible about their enemies before saying, 'Ready-Aim-Fire!'—making them much like the Nazis, after all.

Visitor would have an important initial step to go through with Gorski as part of the *recruitment process*.[§] Visitor had to be confident, first of all, that he was not already a spy—for the Russians! There is nothing worse in the world of intelligence operations than making the mistake of letting your enemy put one of their men inside your own *network*[¶] or organization. Yes, thinking a man is on your side—but having him really working for the enemy—is the greatest mistake an intelligence officer can make. So, how would Visitor make sure Gorski would be on our side and not already working secretly for Moscow?

Well, he would do three things. He would, of course, get to know Gorski in their meetings together and see whether the Polish Officer looks, speaks and acts like a *reliable*** and not a

---

* Collected: Having control over your emotions. Able to seem relaxed when you are in real danger.
† On their turf: In their country.
‡ Torture: Hurt someone very badly trying to get information.
§ Recruitment Process: The organized steps that go into getting a person to agree to be a spy.
¶ Network: The group of intelligence people working against the Russians.
** Reliable: A person who could be trusted to do what is right and what he has agreed to do.

bad or *unreliable** person. Visitor would ask himself, "Does what Gorski is revealing to us now make sense with everything we already know about him?" Dr. Kaminski, of course, had spoken highly of Piotr Gorski and said he owed the Polish Officer his own freedom. That was a good beginning.

The next thing Visitor would do is get Gorski to tell Visitor about *important, secret things happening in Poland*—things the Russians would not let him expose if he were *under their control.*[†] The Americans had to be sure, then, this was not a *dangle operation*[‡] in which the Russians present a fake possible spy who is entirely under their orders and direction. Dangle operations can make a spy organization waste a great deal of time. It also can expose some of their own secret agents and secret techniques to the enemy. As added protection, Visitor would have Gorski take a *polygraph*[§] or *lie-detector*[¶] exam. This would be done to see whether Gorski was trying to deceive the Americans on important things such as working secretly for the Russian Secret Police.

Visitor knew that by the time he had spent several hours with Gorski doing all of the above, he would be able to judge very well whether Gorski should be recruited, trained and return to Warsaw as a trusted secret agent. If the answer turned

---

* Unreliable: A person who cannot be trusted.
† Under their control: Really working as a spy for the Russian Secret Police.
‡ Dangle Operation: Just as one may hang a shiny object in front of a baby to get its attention, intelligence services sometimes make it look like a person is willing to work for the enemy when, the whole time, he is just fooling or deceiving them.
§ Polygraph: A machine that measures the heart, breathing, skin reaction to test a person for honesty.
¶ Lie-detector: The common name for a polygraph machine and test.

out to be yes, then Visitor would get Gorski trained thoroughly in *secret communications** which is what the Polish Major would require to report on secret things without being caught by the Russians back in Warsaw. After all, once he agreed to spy for America, Gorski's own safety would become the U.S.'s highest responsibility. He would be a member of the American team—an ally—one of the family, so to speak. In sum, Visitor had to be very thorough in *screening*† the Polish Major now so everyone later on was not terribly sorry.

Getting down to business, Matt Hale and Visitor examined the papers David had delivered, which were proving to be quite helpful. To begin with, the papers showed that Major Gorski in his security duties at the Vienna Conference would be busy during the day and occupied watching over the delegates long into the nighttime hours. The papers that David brought back informed the Polish delegates that, if they had any problems, they should contact Polish Major Gorski at his room in the Red Storm Hotel, "room number 7 on the first floor." Delegates were told to contact Russian Major Ivan Volkov in room number 11 on the second floor if they had any problems with Russian officials in Vienna. The schedule showed that the only time Gorski might be safely contacted by Visitor would be after midnight. At other times, Gorski might be spotted with Visitor by other delegates—or even worse, by the Russian, Major Volkov.

---

* Secret Communications: All the things a secret agent might need to be trained in, such as secret writing, clandestine photography, short-wave radio, dead drops or hiding places, and secret signals to be able to report to the American intelligence officer he would be working with inside Poland.

† Screening: Complete and careful examination of a person's background and suitability for a job.

Major Volkov was, in fact, a member of the Russian Secret Police. He had been sent to Vienna from Warsaw to keep an eye on the Polish delegates as well as on Gorski. It was all part of the Russian Secret Police program to tighten its *grip** on the Poles—especially on those working for them in matters of security. So, it was decided in Visitor's discussion with Matt Hale that he would go into the Red Storm Hotel after midnight that night—he would arrive there *in disguise,*† dressed as a plumber repairman. Because most of the old Vienna hotels had problems with their pipes, faucets, and toilets, it would not be cause for surprise that a plumber would show up even at that late hour.

Visitor would knock on Gorski's door at 12:15 am and *address*‡ him with a Polish greeting and hand Gorski a handwritten note from the scientist recently rescued by the Hales up in Linz. The note would say that Visitor too is a 'friend of Chopin' who wanted to meet Gorski and say hello. As a Security Officer himself, Gorski would have a pretty good idea almost immediately what Visitor really wanted. The Major would either welcome Visitor or, if he were afraid even to talk, probably say he was busy and not interested. The first contact between the Polish Officer and the American spy would be no more complicated than that.

Visitor was thinking that one of the good things in going after an intelligence or security officer in the spy business is the *efficiency*§ of it all: the fellow being contacted *grasps*¶ immediately what is happening and has a good idea which intelligence

---

* Grip: Control over.

† In disguise: With a change or look or appearance such as wearing a wig or wearing a worker's clothes.

‡ Address: Speak to.

§ Efficiency: Can be done rather quickly.

¶ Grasps: Understands immediately and without explanation.

service is interested in him. This saves time and is quite effi-
cient. So, as he walked out of the Hale hotel, Visitor was feeling
pretty good about things. David and Thor, *coincidentally,** were
arriving back from their walk around town. Visitor told the boy
he had left him something to practice with in the city and that
his dad would tell him all about it.

When David and Thor reached the room, Matt Hale greeted
his son with a big smile and said that the papers David brought
from the Red Storm Hotel were helping Visitor *considerably.†*
They had saved an entire day, at least, which was important
for Visitor who had barely five or six days to carry out an important operation. Matt Hale then told David he had a couple
of neat cameras David might like to use. One, a gift to the boy
from Visitor himself, was the latest 35-millimeter camera—the
Leica 3c. That brought a smile to the boy's face as he picked up
the prized German camera and read the tag—"For DH, Best
Photo Guy in all of Austria."

The junior spy then told his dad that, as he was approaching
their hotel, he saw something odd. A Jeep was parked across
the street—it had soldiers—four in all—each one wearing a
completely different uniform. "The driver was an American—I
could not tell for sure about the others. But one looked like a
Russian!"

Matt Hale explained that these were known as *Four Men in
a Jeep.‡* Yes, these were all soldiers and there was an American,

---

*   Coincidentally: Just happened to be.
†   Considerably: Very much; a great deal; a lot.
‡   Four Men in a Jeep: To keep peace and quiet in the International
    Zone in downtown Vienna, the Jeep carried four military police of-
    ficers including an American, an Englishman, a Frenchman and a
    Russian.

an Englishman, a Frenchman, and yes even a Russian. They patrolled downtown Vienna—the International Zone—like policemen. How Austria ended up with such an unusual situation—rather than the Viennese running their own city—is quite *complicated*."*

Four Allied Soldiers in Jeep Policing Central Vienna

---

* Complicated: Not easy to understand.

4

Austria: The *Occupied** Decade

The senior spy went on to explain how it all started in 1943 during World War II when the Allies met in Moscow, Russia in a conference to reach an agreement on how they would manage things across Europe once they had defeated Nazi Germany. Austria presented a *unique†* situation. It had been the first country Hitler's Nazi Army invaded when, in March 1938, they marched into the nation and forced the Austrians to give up their independence and become part of Germany. After being *forcibly‡* made part of the Nazi Third Reich, a million Austrians went on to fight on the Nazi side in World War II. *Regardless,§* because Austria had in fact been invaded in the first place, the Allies decided to treat Austria after the war as the first victim of Nazi Germany—and not the same as they would treat Germany itself. It was agreed, instead, to set up special rules that would help Austria recover from the war and be treated in the future as victims of Nazi Germany, and not enemies of the Allies.

At the same time, back in Moscow, Russian leader Josef Stalin directed his intelligence and security services to go after

---

* Occupied: When foreign armies are in control of a country, in this case Austria.

† Unique: Like no other; unusual; one of a kind.

‡ Forcibly: Not freely but, instead, under extreme pressure.

§ Regardless: Even though; despite the fact that.

America which he *declared** was the new MAIN ENEMY of the Communist world. So, at the very time America and Russia were supposed to be Allies and the Americans were sending to Russia hundreds of supply ships loaded with free military materials and food to carry on their fight against Nazi Germany, Communist leader Stalin in fact was himself preparing for post-war conflict against The West.

The practical difficulties in dealing with a false ally like Russia really started to become *crystal clear*† two years later, in 1945. This was when the Russian Red Army—the first Allied army to reach Austria—began their bloody assault on Vienna. The Russians, attacking from the east, soon captured the Austrian capital city but only after losing thousands of soldiers in the battle. That was in April. Attacking from the west and north, the American and British Armies reached the northern and western parts of Austria later on. The Americans arrived in July and the British in September. By the time the Americans and British got into Vienna in the east of Austria, the Russians were well *advanced*‡ in their program to steal and send to Russia everything they could get their hands on—not just in Austria, but in every country they conquered on their way to their final destination, the Nazi Germany capital of Berlin.

The Russians were very *aggressive*§ and *bullied*¶ the British to turn over to the Red Army and Russian Secret Police many

---

* Declared: Strongly said.
† Crystal Clear: Just as clear as looking through a washed fine glass.
‡ Advanced: Far along.
§ Aggressive: Pushy, forceful.
¶ Bullied: Pushed around and took advantage of them.

thousands of refugees, including *Cossacks** who had fled Russia back in 1918, after fighting the Communists during the Russian Revolution. Knowing the evils of Communist Russia, the Cossacks would later fight on the German side in WWII. Once in Russian hands as prisoners, the Cossacks were murdered in great numbers—especially their leaders. The rest were shipped like cattle to the most *remote†* Russian region in the frozen north.

Back in Vienna, the Soviet *replacement‡* troops, who came into Vienna after the Red Army fighting had ended in April, were out of control—raping Austrian women as well as killing and robbing the local citizens. Because of the *bad conduct§* of their soldiers, the Russian leaders soon realized they could never control the Austrian population as completely as the Red Army and Russian Secret Police had been able to do in the rest of Eastern Europe. This was clearly demonstrated when the Austrians voted in their first free and open election—the Russian-supported Communist Party of Austria won only five percent of the votes. Seeing how much they were despised by the Austrians, Russia's leaders in Moscow finally agreed with America and the British to allow the Austrians to regain their independence after ten years—in 1955.

That agreement required that, after 1955 when the Allied troops all left the country, Austria would thereafter be *neutral¶*

---

* Cossacks: A fierce tribe of warriors in Central Europe who were famous for their skill as horsemen and warriors.

† Remote: Far away from their own lands or the major cities of Russia.

‡ Replacement: Those who took the place of the Battle of Vienna fighting troops.

§ Bad conduct: Terrible behavior and way of acting.

¶ Neutral: Not on either side; independent.

between Russia and The West. The Russians did not get all that they really wanted—to turn Austria into a Communist nation. Yet, in the end, Moscow came away with billions of dollars' worth of stolen machinery, food and industrial goods. They also got the assurance that Austria would remain neutral and independent in the *Cold War** that began as soon as WWII itself had ended. The Russians knew from 1943 onward that they were going to be in a new kind of war—this was a reality that leaders in The West still had not yet realized or so far figured out.

It would take until 1946—and an important *Telegram*† from the American Embassy in Moscow—to awaken and convince America's political leaders back in Washington that they were indeed in a new kind of struggle, now against Communism— one so serious and dangerous in fact it had to be treated as a war. This life and death *competition*‡ would hopefully not become a shooting or a *Hot War*§ like the first two World Wars where millions were killed. It would be a *"Cold War"* in which spies would play an important role as The West faced an enemy more dangerous than any they had faced in the past.

An American *diplomat*¶ in Moscow, George Kennan, wrote and sent what became famous and known as the "Secret

---

*   Cold War: The strategic struggle between East and West—Russia and America/England—that started in the mid-1940s and lasted till the Soviet Union collapsed in 1991.
†   Telegram: An electronic message more or less like an email.
‡   Competition: Struggle against each other—West against East.
§   Hot War: Where countries and armies fight an enemy using bombs, missiles and guns.
¶   Diplomat: A person sent by the State Department overseas, in this case to Moscow to work in the embassy and deal with the Russians.

Telegram" or "Long Telegram." He had been asked by the Treasury Department in Washington to explain why the Russians had become so opposed to joining America, England and other countries in a partnership to help in the recovery program for nations damaged severely in the war. Kennan wrote back an 8,000 word reply that explained the background and hostility of Stalin's Russia and, in the report, alerted leaders in America that The West indeed had a very serious "Russia problem." In his well-written and *persuasive** report, he succeeded in convincing America to change its ways in dealing with this new and dangerous threat from Communist Russia. Like Nazi Germany back in the 1930s, the Communist Russians were showing they too wanted to take over Western as well as Eastern Europe. Kennan argued that America and its allies in The West had to develop a Policy of Containment to keep Russia from conquering more lands and leading the world into World War III.

Speaking to his son this July day in 1947, Matt Hale predicted that the Cold War in the end will be won or lost—not mainly because of bombs and guns—but because of ideas and the *commitment*[†] needed to hold back the Russians until their terrible Soviet system collapsed. Matt Hale explained further, "because the Russians use subversion, terror and *deception*[‡] as their *principal*[§] ways of dealing with other countries, America must use its own secret intelligence operations and spies to make absolutely sure our leaders know what the Russians are

---

*   Persuasive: One that informs and changes minds.
†   Commitment: Strong intention and willingness to fight to remain free.
‡   Deception: Misleading, lying, fooling.
§   Principal: Most important.

doing and be equally sure they do not succeed. And, Son, this means you and I must help Visitor in every way possible—what he is doing is terribly important."

Matt Hale then told David that he should use the afternoon to get to know Vienna better and become familiar with his new camera. "After all, Son, our brain can *record and recall** only so much information—so few images. There is nothing better than black and white *35-millimeter film†* to do a spy's job. The new color films give us pictures that are pretty, but they are not nearly as good in our "special work." A black and white photograph has more *detail‡* than color photos. Take Thor with you and then you won't have to worry about getting robbed. I know that both his black fur and white teeth look scary to most strangers. Here, use this little carrying bag for the camera and it will be less visible to any thieves and pickpockets in downtown Vienna."

"And look, Son, let's see whether you can become an expert in the downtown area itself. If so, that could be very helpful. How about I test you on this Vienna city map later on? If you impress me with what you have learned, we'll head over to the Sacher Hotel for a slice of '*Sacher Torte.*'§ That hotel is now the headquarters in Austria for our friends, the British. By the way, stay away *altogether¶* from the Red Storm Hotel. If you are spotted around there a second time, even those sleepy security

---

*   Record and Recall: Remember later on.
†   35-Millimeter Film: The most common standard film size in the world at that time and for years afterwards.
‡   Detail: Information.
§   Sacher Torte: World famous chocolate cake with a layer of apricot jam in the middle.
¶   Altogether: Entirely, completely.

guards may start wondering about you. See you at 6:00." David listened intently to his dad the whole time he spoke—not saying a word. Trying to become a better listener, he just nodded and gave a *crisp** military response—*"Aye, Aye, Sir."*[†]

Matt Hale smiled while winking at the boy and thought how lucky he was that David had wanted to spend the summer with him. Real lucky. Later on, at 6:00 o'clock *sharp,*[‡] father and son met up and reviewed the city map together. It was clear at this point that David was getting a good grasp of how Vienna had been designed and knew the locations and layouts of the interesting buildings, parks and public gardens, just as his dad had suggested. The two then walked over to the Sacher Hotel and had a small plate of *Hungarian Goulash*[§] followed by a slice of their famous cake. It was such a good meal.

---

*   Crisp: Neat, smooth, fast.

†   Aye, Aye, Sir: In the Navies of both England and America, it means the speaker understands what he has been told to do, and he will do it immediately and exactly as ordered.

‡   Sharp: Exactly.

§   Hungarian Goulash: A beef and vegetable dish of food with a rich gravy. Hungary is on the eastern border of Austria and, like Poland and so many other nations of Eastern Europe back in 1947, would soon find itself under the control of Russia's Secret Police and the Red Army.

Dressed as a Plumber, Visitor Contacts Gorski

5

Visitor Meets Gorski

The Date: July 9, 1947
Early Wednesday, After Midnight

If Visitor's own mother had been standing in front of the Red Storm Hotel that same evening when the clock struck midnight, she would not have recognized her very own son walking past her and *strolling** in the hotel front door that led to the lobby. He wore the clothes of an Austrian *tradesman*† and carried a plumber's bag of tools. Wearing both a grey wig and *unkempt*‡ moustache, he looked much older than his thirty-three years.

As he went past the front desk clerk, Visitor spoke just three words in German: "Toilet, room seven." Visitor then headed down the *corridor*§ to the right as though he had been there before. The hotel lobby was crowded with drunk or nearly-drunk conference delegates loudly returning from another night on the town. Some needed help finding their rooms. The busy front desk clerk paid no further attention to Visitor; he would not even recall later on that some old plumber had been there or where he had gone. At this late hour he just wanted to get

---

* Strolling: Walking in a calm relaxed way as though he were out for a Sunday walk.
† Tradesman: The working clothes of a man who made or fixed things.
‡ Unkempt: Sloppy looking and not nice and neat.
§ Corridor: A long hallway with many rooms on either side.

all the Russian and Polish drinkers quickly back to their own rooms so none would get sick in the lobby and *puke** all over the place—he was so tired of cleaning up after them.

The hotel guest in Room 7—Major Gorski—was glad it was past midnight. It meant that all or almost all of the Polish delegates were back in their rooms. The chances were good, then, he would get a good night's sleep himself—assuming he could get to sleep. Major Piotr Gorski was a deeply tired man—*physically*[†] and *mentally*.[‡] He was tired of taking care of grown men who did not just get a little drunk—they drank more than they could handle so they would get very drunk. Gorski was sick of many things—from his Polish bosses back in Warsaw to—as he privately called them—'the rotten Russians' who treated him and the other Poles more like prisoners of war than like allies.

And he was *stressed*[§] by his family situation. Since his wife died in the bombing in the war, he had barely managed to care for his two children. He was fortunate that he had the help of his sister who lived outside the city of Krakow in western Poland. This was not far from the border of Czechoslovakia. She had been raising them since he lost his wife, as though they were her very own children. Major Gorski did not want them brought up as little Communists, as he would have been forced to raise them if they were with him. He personally had behaved with the Russians as though he were a loyal Communist—so

---

*   Puke: Throw up, vomit.
†   Physically: In his body and how strong and healthy he felt.
‡   Mentally: In his mind and how rested and clear-headed he was his thinking.
§   Stressed: Pressured, worried, not at peace.

far they seemed to believe this act. After all, to get on better terms with the Russians, he had joined the Polish Communist Party—a move that probably saved his job security, and even his own life.

It was a move that made him feel deeply ashamed whenever he thought of his childhood friends who were murdered by Russian death squads early in the war. Yes, they had been the true Polish heroes and innocent victims. Yet Gorski wanted to believe he had no other choice—he had to stay alive to protect and support his two children. At least that was what he told himself. But, when alone and thinking about his life, about his wife or just saying a prayer, he would occasionally beg for God's forgiveness because he had not fought the Russians as so many of his Polish pals had done.

Without saying a word to anyone, Gorski secretly *mused** that he and his children might someday get away from the Russians—to Austria or Italy or possibly to the American city where so many of his childhood Polish friends had gone— Chicago! That was his dream. For a hobby—and to keep up his own spirits—he had memorized almost all the street names and their locations in the *Windy City*,† as though he would get there—some day—somehow.

And now, just when he was ready to take off his shoes and try to get to sleep, he got a knock at his door. "What a long, long week this is going to be," he thought. He went over, opened the door and found a stranger standing there with some

---

* Mused: Dreamed or privately wished for in his mind.

† Windy City: Nickname for Chicago because of the breezes and strong winds that come off Lake Michigan.

kind of workman's bag in hand. Visitor started to enter—Gorski blocked his way. He had learned under the Germans and then from the Russians not to trust anyone. So first he demanded to know exactly who this man was and what he wanted at this late hour of the night. He started speaking to the stranger in German, "Can I help you, Sir?"

But he got a shock when the old man with the bag looked at him, smiled and spoke to him in perfect Polish, "Major Gorski, Piotr, I come as a friend of Chopin. I need to speak with you about the future—Poland's and yours. If necessary, I can return tomorrow night instead." Visitor then handed Gorski a note written in Polish from the Major's old friend, Dr. Kaminski, saying "Thank you, Piotr—all is well."

As much and as long as Major Gorski had been hoping for this day to come, he was *stunned** and too nervous to remain standing. He pulled Visitor in by the arm and quickly shut the door. He felt unsteady and sat on the bed. For a few seconds he could think of nothing to say.

To begin with, he was deeply *concerned*† that Major Volkov, the Russian, might show up at his door and discover this stranger whom Gorski could not explain. As he did his best to calm down the Polish officer, Visitor went into the bathroom and immediately flushed a huge wad of toilet paper and small cloth that clogged the toilet and sent water flowing all over the floor.

Looking at Gorski with a wink and a smile, Visitor said, "Relax, Piotr. A plumber like me only gets called when things

---

*   Stunned: Shocked, bewildered.
†   Concerned: Worried, afraid or fearful.

are messed up. And, right now, Poland is really messed up and you know that as well as anyone. Anyone coming to the door will find me working to unclog things before the entire first floor gets flooded. Even Volkov the *Ruskie** will agree that a clogged toilet calls for a plumber and needs to be fixed. Besides, Piotr, my friends told me before I came here that Volkov tonight looked like he had drunk a great deal of vodka this evening and had to be helped back to his room. So don't worry—he is sleeping like a *detka*[†] and a danger to no one."

Gorski nodded in agreement, figuring that this guy understood his situation. Meanwhile, water from the overflowing toilet was running all over the room as Visitor flushed the clogged-up toilet for a second and then a third time. Visitor grinned at Gorski and *assured*[‡] the Polish officer that he would clean up the mess before he left.

"Right now," Visitor said, "let me tell you why I am here and it has to do with one thing and one thing only—freedom. We know—and by 'we' I mean we Americans—that the Russians are quickly turning your country as well as many others into slave states, *period.*[§] If you, Piotr can accept slave states, then I should just clean up the water here, say goodbye and go on my way. But, if you ever want to see a free Poland again, then maybe you can help make that happen by working with us. As you have certainly figured out by now, this—intelligence—is

---

* Ruskie: Nickname for a Russian and, during the Cold War, not a favorable one.
† Detka: "Little baby" in Russian.
‡ Assured: Promised.
§ Period: The end of a sentence usually but in this case it is a way of ending it more strongly.

my business and I will make sure, Piotr, that you are safe. That, Piotr, is what I do."

At this point, Gorski, who thought he already understood what Visitor was going to ask him to do, *blurted out** that he could not *defect*[†] and stay in The West. He said he had family members back in Poland who needed his support and protection. "Yes, from the rotten Russians. I must go home." As Gorski spoke these words, tears *welled up*[‡] in his eyes. He, like so many parents around the world, cared first and foremost about his own son and daughter—his Jan and his Karina—ages 11 and 8. So, Gorski thought to himself, "Although this American might give me a way to escape the Communists, I cannot walk away from my children and leave them there."

Visitor did not respond right away. He could tell that Gorski was having a difficult time *emotionally*[§] with all the pressures he was under. Visitor went back to unclogging the toilet, giving the Polish Major some moments to recover so their discussion could continue. Then Visitor walked over to Gorski and put his hand on the man's shoulder, looked him in the eyes and said that they had no *intention*[¶] of asking him to not return to Poland. In fact, defecting to The West was the last thing the Americans wanted at this time. "We actually want you to go back to Warsaw, Major Gorski. In Poland you can help not only your country but also the entire world. You can give your

---

*   Blurted Out: Said suddenly and emotionally, with feeling.
†   Defect: Leave the Communist world and live in The West helping the Americans against the Communists.
‡   Welled Up: Flooded his eyes.
§   Emotionally: In his feelings.
¶   Intention: Wish or desire.

children a better future—with our help. Let's calm down a bit and talk. I promise you I will get out of here in the next couple of hours. First, we need you to clear up some things that, at this point, I do not yet fully understand."

Gorski had settled down *enormously** now that he *grasped*[†] that Visitor did not want him to defect alone to The West—as much as the Polish Major wanted someday to get to Chicago. For the next two hours, the men had a thorough discussion. Visitor had to *determine*[‡] two important things—first, whether Gorski really was a reliable person—meaning not working for the Russians—and, second, that he was *solid*[§] enough *mentally*[¶] and emotionally to work as a spy back in Poland where the dangers were enormously great.

Visitor began by asking Gorski to explain why he had joined the Communist Party and how he had been able to get the Russians to trust him—unless of course he was really on Russia's side. The Polish Major spoke freely and made it clear that he joined the Communists because he knew he could be killed if he did not. When he took this step, his wife had already died. He knew that he would be the only one who could protect and support their children—assuming the Russians did not execute him as they were doing to so many Poles under their control.

Visitor told Gorski that he believed him to be a patriotic

---

* Enormously: Greatly.
† Grasped: Understood.
‡ Determine: Figure out or clarify.
§ Solid: Strong, steady, stable.
¶ Mentally: In the clarity and common sense of his thinking and in his mind.

Pole. But, because Visitor was working against Communists—
for whom truth is not important—everyone working in their
special work had to be tested thoroughly. That meant he would
have to pass a polygraph exam. The test, said Visitor, would
help prove that Gorski could be trusted to do secret work back
in Warsaw. "In fact," said Visitor, "we have to get that step over
with soon—if at all possible, tomorrow night after midnight."

Gorski agreed to do so. He added, "Tomorrow night will
be fine so long as Volkov has another busy night of drinking
vodka and does not come to my room—drunk or half drunk."

Visitor said his friends would make sure Volkov got a few
free drinks to ensure Gorski's safety. Visitor then said, "Look
Piotr, tell me about the Russians in Warsaw. Who is the head of
Russian Security in Poland? Is he in the *NKVD** or the *GRU*?†
I need the names of the top Russian intelligence and security
operatives in Warsaw. Tell me about the Red Army tank and
troop units in Poland. Tell me about the tanks themselves.
Which model tanks? How many do they have and where are
they located? Which cannons are on the new tanks? Tell me
the names of Russia's key military officers in Poland. Where
are the Red Army military storage areas? Tell me the plans the
Russians in Poland have in case there is a war."

And, so it went—for two hours Gorski answered all of
Visitor's questions one by one while Visitor took extensive
notes. When his watch showed it was three o'clock, Visitor
thanked the Polish Major and said, "I am proud of you, Piotr—
as a man and as a Polish patriot. I hope things will work out.

---

*   NKVD: The Russian civilian spy agency later called the KGB.
†   GRU: The Russian military intelligence agency.

And, Piotr, I hope you know that you can quit working with us at any time that you wish. Unlike the Russians, we are not in the business of *blackmailing** people to help us out. When you work with us, protecting your personal safety and freedom begins immediately—and it will not end. We will talk tomorrow night about your two children—when the polygraph is over—on how we might help them. And Piotr, do not write anything down that we have discussed or you think might be of interest to me. The Russians here in Vienna have very great *capabilities.†* They may even go through your room while you are gone for the day. Good night my friend. See you tomorrow night."

---

*   Blackmailing: Forcing a person to do something he does not want to.
†   Capabilities: The ability to do things. Including spying in hotels, following people, listening in on phone calls.

David Enters Red Storm Hotel, Russians in Lobby

6

Recruitment Is a Team Sport

The Date: July 9
Daytime Wednesday

All three of the American players in the Polish Major *recruit-ment activity** were busy this third day of the operation. After leaving the Red Storm Hotel in the early morning hours, Visitor had returned to the Intelligence Group at the Vienna office and wrote his report on the Gorski meeting, as well as relayed the information Gorski had provided on the Russian tanks and battle plans in case of war. He left a copy for the Intelligence Group Chief and sent a copy *electronically*† to Washington. By the time Visitor finished all of this, the sun was rising over Vienna. He drove to the Hale hotel and, although he had not slept, was feeling pretty good. Later, probably around mid-day or early afternoon, he would need to get a couple of hours of *shut-eye*‡ if he were going to able *to function*§ well with Gorski again after midnight tonight. But, he needed first to meet with Matt Hale and tell him how the meeting with Gorski had gone.

---

*   Recruitment Activity: The complete steps being taken to get a person to agree to work as a spy.
†   Electronically: By a radio message which was encoded so that the Russians could not read it.
‡   Shut-eye: A slang word or term for sleep.
§   Function: To work well and be awake and alert.

By the time Visitor got to Matt Hale's room, David had already gone out and was taking pictures with his new camera and sack full of new film. Thor went along and provided protection from any early-morning thieves. Yes, it was a new war—a Cold War—a new enemy—the Russians—and Thor was on patrol once again.

So far, in Visitor's mind, things were moving along quite well. But, there was still some work to do to make sure he was not being fooled by the Russians. The polygraph exam tonight would help *confirm** whether Gorski was being entirely honest—or not. Meanwhile, Visitor was somewhat concerned there might not be enough time to train Gorski fully and properly in the various types of *clandestine commo technologies†* that would *enable‡* the Polish Major to pass secret information to the American contacts when he got back to Warsaw.

Visitor then asked Dr. Hale if he could think of any reasonable medical way that would allow Gorski to remain in Vienna for another week—but be able to do so without placing the Polish Major *under suspicion§* with the Russians.

"And I do not mean running him down with a car, Matt," joked Visitor. "After all, we aren't the Russians. No, we need him to delay his return to Warsaw, if it is possible—for two reasons. First, the security situation in Warsaw is getting very bad, making our work there highly dangerous. So, Gorski needs to be well trained to survive as a long-term clandestine reporting

---

*   Confirm: Help know for sure.
†   Clandestine Commo Technologies: The many ways for a spy to send and receive messages; for example, radio messages, photographs, secret signals on the streets of Warsaw, dead drops for hidden messages.
‡   Enable: Allow or permit.
§   Under suspicion: Where they do not trust him.

source. Second, Gorski is already showing signs he could very soon become a most valuable secret agent. His *access** to senior officers of the Russian Army in Poland is excellent. Almost none of the Russian colonels and generals speaks Polish—they rely often on Gorski to translate for them. That puts him in a superior position to report to us on Russian *military intelligence*."†

Visitor continued, "Our Intelligence Group here in Vienna, I am sure, will be highly impressed with Gorski's *potential*‡ and by the information he gave me last night. I am confident we will soon hear back from the *Pentagon*§ in Washington that the Generals there feel the very same way—that Gorski, in a short period of time, has reported some great stuff."

Dr. Hale sat back in his chair and thought a while before answering. He responded that he might have a way to delay Gorski's departure. He wanted to join Visitor in tonight's meeting—after a successful polygraph test—to examine the Polish Major physically and find out about Gorski's *general health*¶ and see whether he already had his *appendix*** or *gall bladder*†† *surgically*‡‡ removed.

---

*   Access: Ability to meet important people and learn important secrets.
†   Military Intelligence: Secret information about armies and war plans of the enemy—in this case, of the Russians.
‡   Potential: How good he could be as a spy in the future.
§   Pentagon: Is the headquarters for the American Military including Army, Navy, Marines and Air Force. Built during WWII as the largest office building in the world, it is also is where America's top generals work.
¶   General health: For his age, is strong, energetic and free of major medical problems.
** Appendix: A small organ in the belly area that sometimes gets infected and must be removed.
†† Gall bladder: A small organ in the belly area that helps digest food.
‡‡ Surgically: When a person has an operation where a doctor operates on him and opens up his body.

"I have an idea that could work. But, I would need to examine him myself to be sure he is healthy enough for surgery. I have an Austrian friend, a *surgeon*,* who might be able to do the operation; his wife, a nurse, would *assist*[†] him. This doctor works in the Vienna General Hospital. He and I worked together on some secret operations in the war; I know we can trust him. Dr. Hans Brandt has removed many hundreds of gall bladders. My guess is that it would take about ten days to two weeks after the surgery for Gorski to be okay to travel back to Poland—giving you the time you need to train him. If we are able to operate on him, we will need his *Blood Type*."[‡] Good luck tonight. I have to get out to my favorite farm and pick up some supplies that could help—assuming Major Gorski still has a gall bladder. If this is so, there is a pretty good chance we are going to take it out!"

The new day had begun quietly for the Hales who arose much earlier than the *majority*[§] of the downtown hotel residents. David awoke first, as usual, and Thor was last. Father and son had a simple breakfast of bread, cheese and cocoa in their *mini-kitchen*.[¶] Thor had a large beef bone that he was happy to chew outside on the hotel porch. The clock showed almost six o'clock when the Hales went on their way. David

---

*   Surgeon: A medical doctor who operates on people and performs surgery.

†   Assist: Help.

‡   Blood Type: The most common blood categories in humans are Type A, Type B, Type AB, or Type O. Your blood type determines which blood types you can receive.

§   More than half of the hotel guests.

¶   Mini-kitchen: A small kitchen inside their hotel room where they could heat up food and simple meals.

Hale decided to use the morning stroll to walk more than a dozen miles around downtown. He and Thor would have covered more ground except there were areas that had blocked streets as the Viennese were still restoring their beloved city from all the bombings of 1945. In Vienna alone, 3,000 bombs fell in the last months of the war—many still lay *unexploded** under shattered buildings and streets. Each such bomb had to be removed carefully so that no one got killed.

The boy and dog started out in the direction of St. Stefan's Cathedral which gave the boy a good *reference point†* so he would know at all times where he was in the city. This *majestic‡* church and *landmark§* in the center of Vienna was still severely damaged from the wartime Russian artillery blasts. However, its tall South Tower had not been destroyed and was quite visible from all parts of the city. David had a map—he had his new Leica C camera—he still did not have a precise plan this morning except that his dad had told him to learn what he could generally about the *layout¶* of Vienna streets, parks and buildings. He also had to practice taking photos with the various camera settings so he would learn how to get good pictures every time—that is, photographs that were not too light or too dark.

Outside photography, after all, is far more complicated than

---

* Unexploded: Did not blow up but were still very dangerous.
† Reference point: Something tall and easy to see from anywhere in Vienna to keep from getting lost.
‡ Majestic: Very special and the kind of place that would be suitable for a king or special events.
§ Landmark: A well-known building, hill, monument or place.
¶ Layout: The design of the city and location of the major streets, avenues, and the small stream running through Vienna.

copying travel documents under a steady bright light in his dad's study as David had done during the Nazi gold *caper*.* David wrote down in his small notebook the *camera settings*† he used so that he could later see how well the camera worked under many different light settings and *shutter speeds*.‡ To be able to compare results *accurately*,§ he took three photos of the same building, bridge, park, or monument at three different camera settings and recorded the numbers in his little book. This system came about when David asked himself before starting out what his dad would do to be sure, at the end of this day or week, that he would have learned as much as possible. He was not of course just another tourist taking photos to show his family and friends. David was becoming a full-fledged junior spy and he had to do his job *just right*.¶

Dr. Hale, for his part, had a busy day as he was juggling his roles as both medical doctor and senior spy. He had started off the day going to the Rothschild Hospital where he worked with refugees who had arrived the previous week from the east. He then had his meeting with Visitor before driving to the countryside where he bought several bags of carrots for use with Major Gorski—assuming that the Polish officer still had his gall bladder. Before going back into Vienna itself, he drove by the Vogels to ask them an important favor: he needed

---

*   Caper: Adventure.
†   Camera settings: Changes that make a camera take lighter, darker or clearer photos.
‡   Shutter speeds: The amount of time the camera eye or lens stays open so the camera can capture the photo.
§   Accurately: Carefully and with precision.
¶   Just right: Exactly and correctly.

them to make a couple of gallons of *concentrated** carrot juice in large milk containers to take with him. It was so *urgent*† he waited until the mixture was ready. Frau Vogel was happy to help. Due to her own military experience in the war, she asked no questions and proceeded to grind up the carrots, adding just enough water to make the juice drinkable. It took over an hour to get it done, so Matt Hale used the time to go up the hill and check out the castle before he headed back into central Vienna.

On his way back to the hotel, Matt Hale dropped by the Vienna General Hospital and had coffee with his friend Dr. Brandt to see whether his Austrian friend could perform the surgery to help keep an "unidentified friend" in Vienna for several days—sufficient time to be trained by Visitor before traveling back to Poland. Dr. Brandt said he would be more than happy to help—he would make sure the patient got treated well and also had plenty of privacy.

So, each of the three—Visitor, Matt Hale and David Hale— had a job to do to help in the recruitment of Major Gorski—to get him ready to return to Warsaw fully prepared to spy and report on the Russians. There were others who would be needed to make this all come together correctly. After midnight tonight, Visitor would bring to Gorski's room the *polygraph operator*‡ to conduct that *pivotal*§ test. And, because Visitor was the best Polish speaker in the U.S. Intelligence Group, he would assist with the polygraph exam so there would be no room for

---

* Concentrated: Very thick pasty mix.
† Urgent: So important it must be done right away.
‡ Polygraph operator: A technical expert who conducts lie detector tests.
§ Pivotal: Absolutely important.

confusion in the polygraph operator asking or in Gorski answering the very important security questions.

Dr. Brandt at Vienna General Hospital would play an essential part by performing the surgery later in the week even though Gorski's gall bladder was most likely working quite well. At this point—with Gorski's own and his children's future freedom and welfare at stake—Dr. Hale was quite prepared to do what he could to get the Polish Major prepared to work safely back in Poland. If Gorski did not want to have the surgery, he would have to return home sooner, but not as fully trained as he should be. Thus, with less than *sufficient** training, he would be under much greater risk of being caught by the Russians and put to death. Gall bladders, after all, are not the most necessary organ—many people have them removed and go on to live long and healthy lives. And that is what Dr. Matt Hale and Visitor wanted for Major Gorski—a long and happy life after he helped the U.S. Government understand what the Russians were doing and planning.

---

* Sufficient: Enough.

Major Gorski Polygraph

7

Major Gorski on 'The Box'

The Date: July 10, Wednesday night/Thursday Morning

As midnight approached, a slight fog blanketed downtown Vienna and created a perfect setting for the city's spies. Yes, like young David Hale in his castle adventures, spies are primarily nighttime actors—they enjoy the protection they get when *visibility** is poor. While hotel guests stumbled back into the Red Storm Hotel from nearby bars, Visitor and the polygraph operator entered the hotel through a rear door, avoiding the lobby entirely. Gorski had made sure that the rear door was unlocked, as Visitor had asked him the previous night. They went to room seven without seeing or being seen by anyone. As Gorski also had been directed the previous night, he had left the shade in his hotel room window half way up so that Visitor would know—before entering the hotel—whether Gorski had anyone in his room and could therefore not be met this evening.

Gorski's spy training for Warsaw was about to begin. Visitor knocked—Major Gorski let them in—the polygraph operator was introduced simply by the alias '*Marco*.' As he had done the night before, Visitor was dressed as a plumber and, immediately

---

* Visibility: Tells how clearly things can be seen because of the amount of available light or such things as rain, fog and sunshine or darkness.

upon arriving in Gorski's room, clogged the toilet with paper and a cloth. With the second flush, water spilled out onto the floor to give Gorski an innocent *cover story** in case anyone came to his room.

Marco set up his polygraph machine which those who are in the spy business simply *refer to*† as "the box." Visitor and Gorski were doing all the talking—Marco knew some German, but not a word of Polish. Three different devices or gadgets were attached to Gorski, who was told that this really was just another medical exam—they were getting readings on changes in his blood pressure and changes in his breathing. Also, the machine would detect any changes in his *perspiration*‡ when he answered questions. People who are nervous or feel guilty sweat more than usual and their hearts pump faster. The polygraph machine records and *calculates*§ all such changes in the body. Finally, to be certain that Gorski had not taken any drugs to try to appear calm to fool the box, Visitor had Gorski pee in a small cup which he covered and set aside to be tested back at the office—that was to be sure the Polish Major was *clean*⁋ and drug free.

The polygraph testing got started around 12:15 am. It was all done by 2:00 am. The questions were read and explained by Visitor who assured Gorski that everyone involved in his case had been tested on the box too—so Gorski should know that

---

*   Cover story: The agreed-upon excuse for a meeting or operational action that will seem innocent and reasonable to outsiders who may be interested in spies at work.
†   Refer to: Call or name something.
‡   Perspiration: Sweating, which can show whether a person being tested is nervous or not.
§   Calculates: Figures out whether a person is telling the truth, or not.
⁋   Clean: Without any drugs in his system to try to fool *the box.*

they were not asking him to do anything that they had not done themselves. The rules and the security requirements were the same for everyone!

The polygraph questions were really of two types—*informational questions** meant to help understand Gorski's life and his security situation so U.S. Intelligence would know how best to support him and keep him safe. And then came *reliability questions*† to help understand his past and present loyalties, and try to figure out how he might act in the future as a secret agent back in Warsaw.

Gorski would be asked whether he had told anyone else that he had been contacted by American Intelligence, that he helped his Polish friend Dr. Kaminski escape from Warsaw, or that his life's dream was *eventually*‡ to get away from Poland with his children and live in The West. It was also important to know what, if anything, he may have told his sister in Krakow. He was asked whether he had ever committed any crimes, stolen any money from his government, from the Russians, or from anyone. Also, had he ever been arrested or put in jail?

The exam went on for close to two hours when, at the end, Marco spoke privately with Visitor and said that there had been no signs of any lying or *deception*§ in the testing: Gorski had passed the polygraph exam so Visitor could now move

---

*   Informational questions: Used to find out things about Major Gorski such as family situation, his work, his schooling, his fellow workers and bosses, what his friends knew about his true feelings.

†   Reliability questions: These used to make sure the subject was being entirely honest and could be trusted to help learn as much as possible about what the Russian and Polish Communists were doing in Warsaw.

‡   Eventually: At some time in the future.

§   Deception: A sign that the person is being dishonest or hiding something.

forward with the *stay-behind operation.** Visitor went over to Major Gorski, smiled and nodded his head to show that all had gone well. He then gave Gorski a *bear hug*[†] while whispering his congratulations.

"Now, Piotr, we have a lot to discuss to get you back to Warsaw properly trained. We need to discuss ways we might in the future get your children out of Poland—maybe even along with your sister, if that is what you and she want. It might be wise to get your family out of Poland before the Russians shut down the borders in both your country and Czechoslovakia which is the best *pathway*[‡] we can use to get them safely out to Austria before borders are closed. Our Intelligence Group *estimates*[§] that within six months the Russians will make their final move to turn both Poland and Czechoslovakia into Communist-controlled nations. If we get your children and sister out of Poland safely, we would settle them here in Austria until you decide that leaving your country is right for you. Keep in mind, the longer you stay in Warsaw reporting to us, the larger your bank account will be when you do leave Poland for good."

Visitor continued, "You should know by all of this that we highly value both you and the military intelligence reporting you can provide. As we put all of this in motion, we want you to agree to remain in Warsaw for at least two years. During that

---

* Stay-Behind Operation: When a spy remains in a country controlled by the enemy, in this case Poland under Russian Communist rule.
† Bear Hug: A really strong hug between very good friends.
‡ Pathway: The route or way that would be used to get them from Poland to Austria.
§ Estimates: Concludes, thinks, figures, or guesses.

time, the United States Government will place each month in a secret U.S. Dollar account—in your *code name**—the salary of a United States Army Lt. Colonel to help you start a new life with your children—when you get out—while they are still young. Finally, if the work we do together in Warsaw is truly successful, we will *resettle*[†] you and your children in the United States—in Chicago, if you so wish. There, you will be able to work and live your lives in freedom. For now, we desperately need *current*[‡] information on the plans and capabilities of the Red Army Forces in Poland as well as in the rest of Eastern Europe.

"Why is all this so important? Because as soon as Germany and Japan were defeated in 1945, America and England immediately—and many believe quite foolishly—returned to their peacetime ways as most of our World War II soldiers became *civilians*[§] once again. They became farmers, teachers, truck drivers, factory workers and millions returned to college under a special program that paid their school expenses so they could prepare to work in the *peacetime economy.*[¶] We shut down our weapons factories, closed most of our military bases and prepared for peace and not *endless war.*[**]"

"On the other hand, Russia did not—in 1945–1946 or even now in 1947—do what America and England were doing when

---

*   Code name: A made-up name that is used to protect Gorski from the Russians.
†   Resettle: Move him and his family permanently to Chicago.
‡   Current: Up to date, this week's or this month's.
§   Civilians: Men and women who are not in military service.
¶   Peacetime economy: The factories and businesses that are not working on military products.
**   Endless war: Fighting and battles that never end but go on and on.

peace came at the end of the war. *On the contrary,** Moscow didn't move to a civilian or peacetime economy. Stalin instead kept much of his enormous Red Army in the countries they had captured in the war. To make things worse, he used his Secret Police to put Communists in charge of governments all across Eastern Europe. It took a while for The West to wake up but, Piotr, you should know that we in America and those in England as well as much of Western Europe are now wide awake to the Russia threat. And, fortunately, the picture is not all bad."

"To begin with, we are no longer fooled by Moscow—we are rebuilding our military forces to keep the Russians contained and unable to expand their empire. The Red Army is an enormous and dangerous threat to the parts of Europe they do not yet control. You and I—and our freedom-loving friends—are going to make sure Russia and its Communist empire do not *expand*[†] any further. The contribution you can now make is to keep The Western leaders informed on what the Red Army and Russian Secret Police are doing in and around Poland. We need your help, Major Gorski, because the Poles need ours. Eventually, I am certain, Russian Communism will fail."

Gorski sat silently in deep thought. He was thinking about his children. He also thought about his childhood friends who were murdered by the Russians at Katyn Forest early in WWII. And he thought how he was being given a chance to fix his life and erase the shame he had felt ever since joining the Communist Party and working with the Russians. Then he spoke from his heart.

---

*   On the Contrary: Quite the opposite, quite differently.
†   Expand: Increase, grow larger.

"This is the first in a very long time that I feel truly alive—like a man—like a Polish patriot and not a rat. So, yes, I will help you. Just tell me, my friend, what I can do. I promise you will not *regret** putting your trust in me. From one Pole to another, I give you my sacred word."

Tears of joy welled up in Gorski's eyes; this time the tears were neither from sorrow nor from shame. Visitor smiled, shook the Major's hand and said, "Okay. Time to get to work. I have a doctor *colleague†* we will call Dr. Polo who needs to check you out and see whether we can come up with a medical excuse to delay your return to Warsaw for ten days so we can prepare you to work safely with our people in Poland. Dr. Hale then arrived at Gorski's hotel room after receiving a *pre-arranged signal.‡*

With the polygraph exam completed, the operator gathered his equipment and headed off back to the Intelligence Group office to write his report on the test results and send them off to Washington. Now it was Dr. Matt Hale—using the alias *Dr. Polo*—who took over the meeting. Visitor again served as *translator.§*

Dr. Hale proceeded to ask Major Gorski basic questions about his personal health history. It was he who needed to *determine¶* whether the Major was a healthy candidate for the gall bladder surgery. Visitor also wanted Dr. Hale's assessment on

---

* Regret: Be sorry for.
† Colleague: A person who works with him in his job.
‡ Pre-Arranged Signal: A sign telling Matt Hale when it is time to come into the Red Storm Hotel.
§ Translator: A person who explains in English, for example, what is being said in Polish.
¶ Determine: Decide.

another important question: whether Major Gorski seemed to have the required intelligence and *strength of character** for the role of secret spy back in Warsaw where the stress and dangers were quite great.

Fortunately, it turned out, Gorski was in excellent health and had never smoked or drunk alcohol. Now in his mid-thirties, he was as healthy as an athlete and Dr. Hale told him so. There was no obvious reason why he would not go through the gall bladder surgery without difficulty. Before leaving, Dr. Hale showed the Polish Major the two *four-liter jugs†* of carrot juice and explained to him why he must drink as much of the liquid as he could *tolerate‡* in the next couple of days. With this drink, his skin would begin to turn a slightly orange color even though the juice in fact was a very healthy drink. Gorski took a small sip and said it tasted pretty good.

After the polygraph and medical exams were finished, Visitor and Polish Major Gorski had some time alone to discuss the *operational climate§* in Warsaw *in some depth.¶* It was Visitor's job to tailor Gorski's training to make him both safe and *productive*** as a reporting source on the Russians in Poland. The

---

*   Strength of Character: The personal toughness, flexibility and instincts.

†   Four-Liter Jugs: Each jug is slightly more than a gallon.

‡   Tolerate: Be able to accept or deal with.

§   Operational Climate: From the point of view of security, this covers all of the risks and dangers that a spy faces when he is working in a particular country or city and trying to keep from getting caught. This includes the police checkpoints where people have to present their travel documents and there are both patrol dogs and surveillance cameras.

¶   In Some Depth: In some detail or completeness.

**   Productive: Able to report on a timely basis to the American Government just what the Russians were doing and planning both in Poland and the rest of Eastern Europe.

good news for Visitor was that Gorski was not like so many people in his position, who were *inclined** to *underestimate†* the spying risks. Instead, Visitor found Gorski *realistic‡* in *grasping§* that Soviet Secret Police control of his country did not come about by accident. On the contrary, the Russian NKVD in 1947 had been in power and had become very good at catching spies since the Russian Revolution and World War I, back to 1918. The Communists in Russia had remained in power for three decades precisely because they had succeeded in capturing and killing so many of their enemies inside the Soviet Union. With WWII over, they were using these same *techniques¶* of terror all across Eastern Europe.

What made the Russians especially dangerous was that they were willing to murder totally innocent people who were no danger to them. The Soviets killed many tens of thousands of innocent people, not for anything they had done but because of each person's family, religion, nationality, or background. So, if a person came from a wealthy family, that was reason enough to arrest them, imprison them in faraway Siberia and simply work them to death in mines and forests without proper food and housing. In Poland and in the other dozen countries Russia had recently conquered, the NKVD was applying all the lessons of counter-intelligence they had learned back in Russia—both during and after the Russian Revolution.

It was well after midnight when the meeting with Major

---

*   Inclined: Having a certain habit.
†   Underestimate: Assuming that things aren't that bad, being too confident and sure of oneself.
‡   Realistic: Having common sense and not a foolish risk-taker.
§   Grasping: Understanding immediately.
¶   Techniques: Tools and practices.

Gorski ended. Visitor had to get back to his office and write his report with the favorable results of Gorski's polygraph and medical examinations. Things were looking really good that the Americans would soon have a new and most valuable spy in Warsaw!

8

*Spycraft** in Vienna

On Thursday morning, David Hale was up early and got ready to do the job his dad had given him: get to know the central zone of Vienna and become skilled in the use of the Leica camera. One thing David would do to avoid attracting any attention would be to sling the camera strap around his neck and let the camera hang down inside his light *windbreaker*.† In this way, the camera would not be visible from the back or from his left and right sides. When anyone walked or stood directly in front of him, the young spy would *refrain*‡ from taking photos until that person was out of the way. In sum, the young spy was developing the kind of *street skills*§ needed to assist his dad or Visitor in downtown Vienna which was loaded with police, spies, *counter-spies*⁋ and soldiers who take notice of anything that looks *suspicious*.**

---

* Spycraft: The basic training in the spy world and the ways spies are kept safe from discovery.

† Windbreaker: A light jacket that one would wear in spring and fall, but not on very hot or cold days.

‡ Refrain: Stop completely until it was safe and no one could see that he was taking pictures.

§ Street Skills: The ability to get his spy tasks done without attracting attention.

⁋ Counter-Spies: Police or security officials in a country trying to find foreign spies.

** Suspicious: Things that looked unusual or different than what one normally sees in Vienna.

Thor, for his part, would basically be *along for the stroll.** The dog had no specific job to do, except one *crucial*[†] one: his duty at all times—both at the castle and on the streets of Vienna—was to protect young David in a city that contained all sorts of criminals and all sorts of risks. These dangers included kidnappers, thieves, murderers and, of course, old Nazis and present-day Communists. Vienna was far more *perilous*[‡] than life had been back in the United States where David, sister, and Mom had lived safely during the war. The good news for David was that, because he had Thor along, he had more freedom to roam around Vienna than other eleven year old boys who did not have the protection and company of a courageous war dog.

By noon, after a few hours of taking snapshots in and around the public parks and monuments, David led Thor back to the hotel where he developed the Leica film to see how well he was doing in shooting photos. Interestingly enough, he was looking forward to his dad's *critique*[§] because he knew it would make him a better photographer and, of course, a more *effective*[¶] junior spy. His dad was waiting in their room. He had just finished writing the medical reports on the morning's hospital visit that included the treatment plan he had to submit on each of the refugees he had examined that day.

Matt Hale looked over each of David's film shots and pointed out which ones were excellent, which ones were only fair and

---

*   Along for the stroll: Out for a pleasant walk.
†   Crucial: Of great importance.
‡   Perilous: Extremely dangerous.
§   Critique: Evaluation of the boy's photography and suggested improvements for his future photo work.
¶   Effective: Better at doing his work.

which shots would not be very useful because they were *deficient** in some way. Overall, the senior spy was impressed by how the boy had followed his directions and clearly had covered several of the city parks and streets in just a single afternoon. In addition, the boy also had taken good notes. The father explained to David how a photo shot was just right or could be improved by using a different camera setting on the Leica or by maybe taking the shot from a different *vantage point.*†

By this time, after casing the central zone of Vienna, the junior spy was becoming quite familiar with the city streets. He also was becoming a *more selective*‡ camera-man than when he had first started. More importantly, he was enthusiastic about the task because, he figured, his dad or Visitor would soon be using his camera skills, not only in practice exercises but on things that really mattered. When the father and son team had gone through all the Leica 35-millimeter photo shots, the senior spy showed David the second camera Visitor had dropped off earlier.

It was a most-special camera known as the *Minox.*§ About the size of a cigarette lighter or small box of matches, this especially-small camera could be held unnoticed in the hand. When

---

*   Deficient: Not too good.

†   Vantage Point: The spot where David was standing or should be standing to take a better photo.

‡   More Selective: Careful about which pictures were worth taking and which ones were not.

§   Minox: Developed in Latvia and first manufactured between 1937 and 1943, it soon became the world's best spy camera. Of exceptional quality, it was expensive and used by intelligence services throughout the world.

he saw the Minox, David's eyes lit up right away. Compared to the Leica, this was indeed a *miniature** camera—an *honest-to-goodness*† spy camera! To David it looked as *sleek*‡ as the German Luger he liked so much. With his eyes wide open and his facial expression showing his enthusiasm, David felt *downright*§ excited as his dad explained that the Minox could do both document photography and take outside shots—the same as the Leica. He was surprised to learn that such a small roll of camera film could capture fifty shots and that the film itself came in a *cartridge*⁋ that was simple to load and unload. His Dad then showed him how to take photos. David was relieved to find out that he would not have to develop the thin ribbon of film that requires special equipment located back at the Intelligence Group Office.

"When can we try it dad? When can I take it out to the parks?" Matt Hale said he would first need to meet with Visitor to get more specific instructions. He did know that Visitor wanted David's help in photographing every park and monument in downtown Vienna—not from a normal distance as a tourist might take a picture. No, Visitor needed very *close-up*** shots taken from a distance of just a few feet. His dad and Visitor figured that David could get that done more securely

---

*   Miniature: Extremely small, tiny compared to others cameras used in most photography.

†   Honest-to-Goodness: The real thing and without any doubt whatsoever.

‡   Sleek: A lovely design that showed it had been created by an excellent engineer.

§   Downright: Completely and absolutely.

⁋   Cartridge: Container that held the film.

**   Close-up: From a short distance of a couple of feet or less.

than an adult could—after all, a boy out walking with his dog attracts little or no attention.

With some free time on their hands before Visitor was scheduled to arrive, father and son headed over to the Sacher Hotel for a late lunch and a slice of the hotel's Viennese pastry. Returning to their own hotel after lunch, the two were soon joined by Visitor who finally had managed to catch a few of hours of sleep. Matt Hale filled in Visitor on how his surgeon friend, Dr. Brandt, was willing to do either gall bladder or appendix surgery—whichever was required.

Visitor addressed David, "How about you and I have a chat about photography in and around Vienna? Your dad tells me you were just given the Minox Camera and have had plenty of practice with the Leica. This special project I want you to do is going to require patience and very *close-up** photography. I do not want you to attract any attention to yourself. We do not want the Russians to notice that you have any special interest in Vienna's parks and its monuments. The Minox, then, is the right camera for certain parts of this task. If you use it carefully, no one should be able to see what you are doing. In fact, it would be good if you bring along the Leica camera as well. Let that one hang around your neck, but just don't use it. Anyone who sees you and Thor will think you are just a kid out with his *pooch*† for a walk. By the way, we will soon go over in detail the special project involving the Vienna Parks. We can do that once it is approved by the American Intelligence Group. I think you will find it quite challenging and interesting. Take care, young man."

---

* Close-up: From very near.
† Pooch: A slang word for a dog.

Then Visitor sat with Matt Hale and went over the next day's operational plan for the Polish Major who had been originally scheduled on the weekend to be taking a train back to Poland. After midnight, Visitor would have another meeting with Gorski to make certain he was ready for the surgery and not *arouse** any suspicion in the Russian Officer's mind. Separately and earlier in the night, Dr. Hale would be having dinner with Dr. Brandt to *coordinate*† the surgery which would take place early on Saturday morning. With Dr. Brandt's wife assisting in this 'emergency surgery,' no one at the Vienna General Hospital would question the surgery itself.

---

*   Arouse: Cause to be noticed or questioned.
†   Coordinate: Making all parts of the operation and surgery come to-
     gether, again without causing any suspicion.

9

Vienna Surgery *With a Twist*[*]

Friday evening at the Red Storm Hotel was more or less a repeat of the first week of the International Conference on Refugee Infectious Disease. The visiting medical delegates from Eastern and Western Europe, including Germany and Austria, had been learning about the latest treatment techniques and medicines that were being used successfully on refugees infected, in many cases, with *multiple*[†] diseases. Dr. Hale was one of the physicians with the most recent direct experience in treating these refugees; the speech he gave and the medical treatment paper he delivered were warmly received by the attending guests. With millions of homeless refugees roaming around Europe, every country in the region was struggling with the *burden*[‡] of feeding, clothing, housing, as well as medically treating, these foreign victims of war. As the Conference concluded, each of the delegates was getting ready to return to his home country better able to deal effectively with the enormous problems in the camps and hospitals where hundreds of thousands of displaced persons still needed help.

Tonight was their last evening in Vienna and the *majority*[§] of the conference visitors were mainly interested in finding a bar

---

* With a Twist: Different from the usual or normal.
† Multiple: More than one.
‡ Burden: High cost and work caring for displaced persons.
§ Majority: More than half.

or restaurant where they could get a good meal and consume plenty of wine, beer, or vodka. The alcohol, they believed, would help them forget at least briefly their problems and other *depressing** stuff they would have to deal with once they got home. That was especially true for any conference visitors from the Eastern European countries still occupied by the Soviet Red Army and harshly controlled by the Soviet Secret Police. By 1947, all across *war-torn*† Eastern Europe, things since the war ended were just getting worse. Why so?

To begin with, across countries to the east of Vienna, the Russians were starting to close down national borders and take control of the local and national governments. In addition, many Eastern Europeans knew friends who had disappeared *without a trace.*‡ Suddenly one morning, some neighbors were gone—a few may have quietly snuck away to freedom in The West. But, many more had been kidnapped by the Russians and sent deep into Communist Russia—never to be seen or heard from again.

By contrast,§ one of the conference delegates was eagerly preparing his return home to Poland and was taking extraordinary steps to do so. Polish Major Piotr Gorski was *setting in motion*⁋ the plan agreed upon with Visitor from the American Intelligence Group. The Polish recruitment operation, in fact, really got into high gear on Thursday night when Gorski began

---

*   Depressing: Sad, miserable and heartbreaking.

†   War-torn: A region with bomb-damaged buildings, roads, bridges, schools and homes.

‡   Without a trace: Where no one had seen the person or family leave the area.

§   By contrast: Instead, on the other hand.

⁋   Setting in motion: Started or began.

drinking carrot juice every half hour to turn his skin an orange color and prepare himself for the required gall bladder surgery.

Early on Friday morning, Gorski contacted the still-sleeping Russian Security Officer, Major Volkov, and told him he was feeling extremely sick and had a deep pain on the right side of his *abdomen*.* Volkov—who had been over-eating and over-drinking all week himself—was not too concerned. He just assumed the Polish Major too was merely dealing with a case of *indigestion*.† All week long, Gorski seemed fine and had been doing most of the security work at the conference. The Russian, on the other hand, had spent much of his week meeting and drinking with Russian military officer friends stationed in Vienna. Realizing that Gorski had done most of the security work all week, Volkov told the Polish Major to take it easy and get some rest.

As it was the last conference day, Volkov contacted each of the delegates from Poland to make sure that none was missing or had disappeared. He was fairly *confident*‡ that all of them would get on the train headed to Warsaw this Saturday because each conference attendee had family members back in Poland who would be *severely*§ punished if a family member defected to The West. Yes, relatives of Poles who traveled abroad were basically *hostages*¶—they were used by the Russian Secret Police

---

* Abdomen: Stomach or belly area.
† Indigestion: Being sick to one's stomach.
‡ Confident: Sure of himself or certain.
§ Severely: Very harshly.
¶ Hostages: People kept prisoner by kidnappers or a police state. In fact, Russians even needed to have and use 'internal passports' in the Soviet Union and had to have government permission to travel from city to city.

to keep these foreign travelers in line and following all the rules. As far as Major Volkov was concerned, things seemed completely normal and under control when he went to his own room and fell fast asleep after midnight.

So, on Saturday morning when he was double-checking to be sure that none of the returning Poles was missing, Volkov went looking for Major Gorski. He asked the two Russian guards in the lobby and learned that Gorski had been taken to the hospital very late on Friday night—but no one had bothered to wake him up and tell him. After he yelled at the guards and threatened to report their failure to advise him, Volkov had the front desk clerk call the Vienna General Hospital. When they finally were able to speak to someone in charge at the hospital, he was told that the Red Storm Hotel guest had gone through emergency surgery in the night and was now resting in the hospital *recovery room*.*

The previous night, as planned, Dr. Brandt had been waiting at the Vienna General Hospital when Major Gorski arrived by ambulance to the Emergency Room. After middle-of-the-night surgery, the Polish Major was transferred to a small clinic across the street in downtown Vienna. By the time Major Volkov even had learned about the surgery, it was time for him to be at the Wien Hauptbahnhof—Vienna's Central Train Station. Volkov, now alone, had to get the all of the Polish conference visitors on the Saturday morning railway car for the 425 mile trip back to Warsaw.

Well, the *deed was done*†—Gorski's gall bladder was *kaput*‡—

---

*   Recovery room: Where patients are kept until they have gotten through surgery.

†   Deed Was Done: When it is too late to stop something from happening.

‡   Kaput: Gone, broken or disappeared.

and the Polish Major was going to be recovering in Vienna for several days and maybe for as much as a week. At this point, Volkov did not give Gorski another thought. Overall, the Russian was feeling content as he did a final *headcount** of the Polish delegates and found that all 27 of them were at the station and ready to get on the late-morning train back to the east. Later in the day, once the railway car crossed the border back into Poland, Volkov looked out the window, took out a small *flask†* of vodka, and drank every last drop. He did not think again about Major Gorski who had helped make Volkov's own stay in Vienna so easy.

For one thing, the Russian was pleased and aware that the Soviet Secret Police and Red Army would soon be imposing very tough rules on the Polish people. The whole idea of *cracking down‡* on the Poles and other Eastern Europeans resisting Russian rule made the Russian Major very happy indeed. While he had not personally participated in the Katyn Forest *massacre§* of Polish prisoners early in WWII, he would gladly have done so if he had been assigned to that operation. Among the Soviet Secret Police officers in Warsaw, Volkov, after all, was widely known as a *hardline§ enforcer*** of the laws and of punishments— he was, in fact, *enthusiastically††* looking forward to the new Soviet policy to crush Polish *resistance.‡‡*

---

*   Headcount: Counting systematically … one, two, three and so on.
†   Flask: A small bottle used for carrying gin, vodka or whisky.
‡   Cracking down: Getting tough with.
§   Massacre: The murder of great numbers of innocent people.
§   Hardline: Very strict and harsh.
**   Enforcer: A person who makes people follow rules and also punishes people who do not.
†† Enthusiastically: With eagerness and spirit.
‡‡ Crushing: Breaking or punishing.

On the other hand, Volkov did not dislike, let alone hate, Major Gorski as he *despised** most other Poles. This was due probably to Gorski's Communist Party membership as well as his natural *survivability trait*[†]—Gorski tended to get along with all people and was not inclined to clash with those different from himself. This, in Visitor's mind, had been one of the *principal*[‡] reasons he was *confident*[§] on the probable success of this operation—to get a spy in Warsaw.

For the first 24 hours after surgery, Major Gorski had been in a very deep sleep in the recovery room clinic across the street from the Vienna General Hospital. Dr. Brandt had chosen this quiet place for recovery because he knew there would be little or no chance the Russians in Central Vienna would know that Gorski was there. Dr. Brandt knew also that his patient would get the rest he needed on the weekend and be available as early as Monday morning to meet with Visitor and begin his operations training.

---

* Despised: Hated or had a terrible, automatic dislike for someone—in this case just about all Poles.
† Survivability Trait: The ability to endure or last when facing difficult or dangerous conditions.
‡ Principal: Main or most important.
§ Confident: Positive or optimistic.

Vienna General Hospital

10

*Stay-Behind Training**

While the Polish Major was recovering from his surgery, and while Russian Major Volkov was traveling back to Warsaw by train, Visitor put together the *covert training program*† for Gorski. Visitor himself would be *conducting*‡ the spy training over the course of the week. The covert training would be conducted in a private wing of the rehabilitation clinic where Major Gorski was recovering from surgery. This was where Dr. Brandt's wife was employed as the senior medical administrator. She would be making sure that the meetings held with Gorski would be done in private. Dr. Matt Hale had not informed his former war-time ally, Dr. Brandt, exactly what was the U.S. Government's interest in Gorski—or even that the Polish Major would be returning to Poland. Nonetheless, by this time in mid-1947, intelligent and *influential*§ Viennese like Dr. Brandt had already made their personal decision to support The West and not the Russians. Dr. Brandt clearly was on the side of The West. By this time in Austria, fortunately, Russian Communists were unpopular as was clearly demonstrated in

---

*   Stay-Behind Training: This is the special preparation given to spies who will be operating inside the enemy camp, or headquarters, and cannot afford to make mistakes that could cost them their lives.

†   Covert Training Program: Secret spy training.

‡   Conducting: Running the training.

§   Influential: Important people with good contacts in Vienna government, politics and police circles.

the country's first post-war election in late 1946 where the non-Communists received over 95% of the Austrian vote.

The five days of training that Visitor planned for Gorski were very *concentrated** because the Polish Major had to be on the train back to Warsaw by the next Saturday morning. It was helpful that Gorski was familiar with the Russians and knew how to avoid problems since he had to deal with them on a regular basis. On Monday, Visitor planned to concentrate on Gorski's own personal safety and security. Now that the Polish Major had shown that he had *indirect access*† to Soviet military intelligence on a *strategic level*,‡ he had to be protected as completely as possible. Because of this, Gorski's personal safety was *foremost*§ in Visitor's operational planning. *The Pentagon*¶ in Washington already considered Gorski to have great *potential value*** as an intelligence source. At this point in 1947—after two years of dealing with the Soviets since the war—the U.S. Government's most important unanswered intelligence question was whether the Soviets would attack and make The West end up in another war—this time, one started by the Russians. What made the matter even more important was that the Soviet Red Army—especially its tank forces—far *outnumbered*†† all

---

*   Concentrated: Given at a rather fast pace.

†   Indirect Access: Which meant that, although he did not get to see important intelligence information of the Red Army, he was in contact with Russian Generals who knew about Soviet war plans and occasionally let him know what was going on.

‡   Strategic Level: In this case, most important intelligence would include war plans of the Soviet Red Army and especially whether they were preparing and taking steps to attack The West.

§   Foremost: The first and most significant step in the training process.

¶   The Pentagon: Built during World War II, the Pentagon is headquarters for all of America's military services.

** Potential value: What intelligence he could provide in the future.

†† Outnumbered: There were far more Soviet tanks than the Americans had in Poland and Eastern Europe.

the armies in Europe, those from America as well as England. Militarily, things looked rather *grim*.*

As a result, Visitor was *crystal clear*† on the great importance of Gorski's safety—he had to do everything he could possibly do to help make Gorski an effective spy. But, equally important was that the Americans must try to keep Gorski from being caught by the Soviet NKVD. So, the first thing Visitor did was establish a 90-day *cooling-off period*‡ during which Gorski was told that—with one very important exception—he must do absolutely nothing back in Warsaw for the next three months that could possibly call attention to himself or accidentally alert the Russian Secret Police. Visitor discussed with the Polish Major that he needed to behave back in Poland exactly the same as he had acted before coming to Vienna. Therefore, if the Russians were to take an interest in him from the viewpoint of security—maybe because he had just returned from Austria where the American intelligence agents were known to be active—NKVD would see nothing new or unusual in Gorski's behavior that would raise suspicions. Later on, after the cooling-off period was over, a suitable *commo plan*§ would be developed that would both protect Gorski and enable him to send intelligence reports to the American Intelligence Group in Warsaw.

---

* Grim: Not very good; in fact quite unfavorable for the Americans and Western Europe.

† Crystal Clear: As easy to see as looking through a sparkling clean window.

‡ Cooling-Off Period: A period of time he would do no spying and no reporting. This was just in case the Soviet Secret Police investigated him after his Vienna visit as a way to be sure he had not been recruited by Western spy services.

§ Commo Plan: This is what spies call the secret communications plan that protects intelligence operations from being discovered by a foreign government, in this case the Soviet Russians.

What, then, was the exception that Visitor wished to discuss? It was pretty *straightforward**—what should or could Gorski do before the cooling-off period ended if he learned that the Red Army was about to attack The West? Obviously, a war between East and West would be *catastrophic.*† The Red Army in Europe at that time was several times larger and probably too strong to be stopped—especially if they made an unannounced sneak attack, one that came without any warning.

Gorski understood this right away. He knew what had happened to Poland back in 1939 when the Nazis sneak-attacked from the west on the 1st of September and the Russians did the same from the east on the 17th. It was not necessary for Visitor to convince Gorski of the seriousness of such an invasion. The Polish Major enthusiastically told Visitor that he would immediately warn the Americans—assuming he had a safe way to do so.

For a moment, Gorski became quiet as he recalled friends he knew who had been killed fighting both the Germans and the Russians. This discussion reminded him that he not only had not fought the Russians—like other, patriotic Poles—but instead had in fact been working with the Soviets in Warsaw since the War. This was a stain on his *conscience*‡ that Gorski very badly wanted to erase. This led to the subject of clandestine or spy communications including signaling devices and shortwave radios that might be capable of telling the Americans of

---

*   Straightforward: Clear, simple, uncomplicated.
†   Catastrophic: Causing countless deaths and destruction as occurred in World Wars I and II.
‡   Conscience: The inner voice that tells a person whether something is right or wrong.

such an attack. As eager as Gorski was to please Visitor, it was Visitor who insisted that Gorski would not be carrying any obvious spy devices or spy materials when he got off the train in Warsaw. Later on, Visitor assured the Polish Major, he would be given the equipment and materials he needed in his secret work ahead. But that would only happen if it were safe to do so.

The rest of Monday was used to review with Gorski maps of Poland and areas where, as far as Gorski was aware, the Soviet Red Army seemed to be concentrating its military forces. Gorski did mention one region in northwest Poland where, it was rumored, the Red Army Generals had been talking privately among themselves about creating a most secret military base that would be used to attack The West. This base was being kept *Top Secret** by the Russian Generals—in fact, that town and military base had been taken off all maps of Poland. Major Gorski only learned of this when he was helping a senior Russian officer with the travel route he would follow for a military inspection.

Borne Sullinowa was a small village in Western Poland almost 300 miles north of the city of Krakow. Before WWII, the town was part of Germany and the Nazis had built a major Army base there. Hitler visited the base on August 18, 1938 and it was used by the Nazi Army to prepare their invasion of North Africa. After Germany lost the war, a large slice of eastern Germany—including Borne Sullinowa and its secret military base—became part of Poland. During the entire Cold War, however, the town and base were kept hidden and treated not

---

*   Top Secret: The highest or most important intelligence information of the government.

as Polish territory but, instead, as a part of Soviet Russia itself. Poles were not allowed to visit there. Its location and role in Red Army war planning were considered 'Top Secret.'

On Tuesday, Visitor spent a great part of the day discussing with Major Gorski what he could do if he learned that Soviet tank and infantry forces were preparing and taking steps to launch an attack on The West. Obviously, that would be critically important information he would be expected to report. After all, and Gorski agreed, it would do no good if he learned about an upcoming invasion but had no practical way to get that *critical** warning to the Americans.

Wednesday's training was all about clandestine communications and how Gorski might be able to report to the American Intelligence Group in Warsaw as well as receive questions and feedback on his reports. The subject of *dead drops†* was discussed at length as Visitor showed sample materials and photos or sketches so that Gorski would be able to use such strategies safely and effectively. Gorski was not too *confident‡* that downtown Warsaw was currently a safe place to use dead drops—the streets, alleyways and fields were constantly changing as refugees and school kids were always picking up trash and litter, thinking the materials might be useful at home. Warsaw, after all, had been badly bombed and shelled by *artillery§* in the war—so, what looked one way today might look entirely different tomorrow.

---

*   Critical: Extremely important.

†   Dead drops: Rocks, tree branches, trash and other secret hiding devices and materials which could be used for Gorski and the Intelligence Group to send messages back and forth with little chance of falling into the wrong hands.

‡   Confident: To be certain or sure of oneself.

§   Artillery: Long guns that shoot explosive shells several miles.

Thursday morning was used to give the Polish Major a course in *Secret Writing** and the use of chemicals to send reports not detectable by postal authorities. If and when the security situation in Poland became clearer—and the Intelligence Group had successfully tested sending secret writing messages out of Poland—Visitor decided it would not be *timely†* enough in Gorski's case, especially if he was trying to send information that the Red Army was getting ready to attack. In this case, Gorski needed to have a practical way to get an *Emergency Signal‡* to the American Intelligence Group. But how?

As they were chatting during lunch, Visitor asked Gorski whether he had a dog and, if so, did he think he could carry with him to Warsaw a simple dog whistle from Vienna. If he had no dog, could he get one? Gorski said he had no dog but could get one when he returned to Poland—after all, there were *stray dogs§* everywhere. A dog would give him an excuse to go for walks around the parks and streets of Warsaw—it could be helpful also in finding acceptable dead drop sites.

By Friday, Major Gorski was well trained in the *principles and practices¶* of clandestine commo even though he had not been able to practice using such tools and techniques on the

---

* Secret Writing: Writing a letter that uses invisible chemicals that are not visible until they are treated with heat or other ways for the hidden message to be read, usually by the spy organization in another country.
† Timely: Rapidly or fast enough.
‡ Emergency Signal: A warning that something terribly important was about to happen—like an invasion.
§ Stray Dogs: Animals that have no owner and are wandering around just trying to stay alive.
¶ Principles and Practices: The rules and the ways of operating secretly and safely (in Poland the Russian Secret Police were everywhere).

streets of Vienna before going home. With so many Soviet intelligence officers in Vienna, and with Gorski just getting over his surgery, it was considered safer to do all the covert training off the streets and *out of the public view.**

It was indeed fortunate that Visitor was there to conduct the training in Polish and to build on the good and growing relationship between them. Why would that be important? Well, the *litmus test*† in spy recruitment and spy training takes place later on, after the trained spy is back in his home country. Then—all alone—the new spy has to face the dangers, pressures and risks that would cost him his life if he is caught. Over the decades of the Cold War, many recruited and trained spies returned to their countries and, although having agreed to report secretly to an intelligence service, they were never heard from again. Instead, they simply ditched or threw away their spy gear in a river and quietly disappeared. They just were too afraid to be spies, after all.

Visitor's participation in the training would turn out to be essential to the success of the Gorski spy operation. For one thing—unknown to Major Gorski at this time—Visitor would soon be transferred to Poland where he would be in charge of all of the American covert operations—he would also be providing direct in-country operational support to the Polish Major. In all of Eastern Europe, history would show, Poland would *in the long run*‡ turn out to be the most important nation in helping stop the *savage*§ Russian bear from devouring Europe entirely.

---

*   Out of the Public View: Where Gorski would not be seen.

†   Litmus Test: Named after the reliable chemistry test for distinguishing acids and bases using litmus paper, a litmus test is a true test or measure of effectiveness.

‡   In the Long Run: Over the course of many years, in Poland's case four decades during which they were occupied and controlled by Soviet Russia, the Red Army and the Secret Police.

§   Savage: Cruel, brutal, uncivilized and very much like barbarians.

Before Visitor and Gorski finished the training, they spent a couple of hours reviewing options in case the Polish Major had to get an emergency signal to the Americans that the Red Army was preparing an attack from their strong base in Poland. Given the fact that there was no safe or reasonable way for Gorski to meet secretly with the Americans in or around Warsaw, it was decided that the best way would be for Gorski to send a signal that an attack was *imminent** by using the silent dog whistle Visitor had given him and that he would be carrying back to Poland. David had donated Thor's dog whistle for the Gorski operation and delivered it to Visitor using the BMW R75 motor cycle with side car to ferry him and Thor to downtown Vienna on Gorski's last night in town. Such a whistle—invented a hundred years earlier—sends an *ultrasonic signal†* that cannot be heard by humans but can indeed be heard by dogs. It also could possibly be detected by the police or Red Army who

David and Thor Deliver Dog Whistle to Visitor

---

*   Imminent: Ready or about to happen.
†   Ultrasonic signal: A higher pitch than humans can hear.

might know that an ultrasound signal had been sent somewhere in Warsaw—but they would have no idea precisely where it was sent from or who had sent it.

Gorski was told he should send it in the evening as he walked along the Vistula River in downtown Warsaw. If the Soviet attack was scheduled to begin in less than 72 hours, Gorski should send a second signal three minutes later. In any case—whether he blew the silent whistle once or twice—he should immediately throw the whistle into the river and walk away into the darkness. At this point, he should take a train to Krakow where he would be contacted at his sister's farm by Visitor himself or another *friend of Chopin** to arrange for their evacuation to Austria.

A full week later than originally scheduled, Major Piotr Gorski went to the Vienna railroad station and boarded the train back to Warsaw. It was July 19, 1947 and, *within,†* he seemed to be a changed man He felt he had *vigor‡* in his walk. He was holding his head high as he took a seat in the section reserved for military officers and senior government officials. He did have some tightness in his bandaged abdomen where once he had *borne§* a perfectly-healthy gall bladder.

Remembering the advice that Visitor had kept repeating—about not drawing attention to himself—Gorski kept from smiling the smile he was feeling in his heart. After all, he was

---

*   Friend of Chopin: The code name first used by Gorski himself to help the Americans contact Dr. Kaminski in Linz.
†   Within: Inside himself.
‡   Vigor: Energy, strength.
§   Borne: Carried.

returning to Poland to work for peace. So, *consciously** and with *determination*,[†] Major Gorski put on the dour, sour, and humorless face of *Soviet Man*.[‡] In crossing the Polish border, he was starting his new career as a secret American spy in *Soviet-occupied Poland*.[§] And, if the Americans with his help learned what the Red Army and Soviet Russian Secret Police were up to, then maybe war could be avoided and East and West might live in peace. If so, it would in good part be due to American leaders having good intelligence from brave spies such as Major Gorski.

---

* Consciously: Completely aware of what he was doing.

† Determination: With the strong intention of hiding his true feelings at that moment.

‡ Soviet Man: An unhappy person beaten down by a heartless Soviet system.

§ Soviet-occupied Poland: From the moment the Red Army came into the country, Poland became a nation totally controlled by the Soviet Russians. In reality, Poland was Poland no longer.

Visitor Trains Gorski in Secret Communications

11

Hide and Seek

As a *wannabe*[*] junior spy, David Hale awoke this late July 1947 morning with his anxiety level climbing again. This was just as it had been right after the Hales had rescued the Polish scientist from the *clutches*[†] of the Soviet Russian Secret Police (Book I, *Escape to the West*). Now, having dealt effectively with the Nazi goons who had returned to the Hale castle in search of buried loot (Book II, *Nazis on the Run*), David found the morning peace and quiet *unsettling*[‡]—again, he was fearful that the spy games may have come to an end and that he would be left with little more than memories because the 'Knights' of Hale castle had slain all the local dragons. Yes, as leaders of dozens of nations grappled with the chaos and *turmoil*[§] of post-War Europe, including Austria's, David secretly was wishing that things would not settle down completely and get fixed too quickly. After all, the recruitment and training of Polish Major Gorski—though pretty darn good—was not sufficient itself to *turn the tide*[¶] and bring the Cold War to a quick and favorable end. Besides, the boy had another month before school began again—he was in no mood to settle for that.

---

[*] Wannabe: A person who 'wants to be' just like someone else, in this case David wanted to be like his dad working for the American Intelligence Group in Austria.
[†] Clutches: Claws or traps.
[‡] Unsettling: Disturbing.
[§] Turmoil: Chaos or messiness.
[¶] Turn the Tide: Reverse or completely alter, change or fix.

Obviously, David Hale was thinking first about his own situation, not the *overwhelming** struggle between West and East—basically, between the Americans and the Russians. The boy wanted to do things spies do. At eleven years old, he was not always able *to see the big picture*† as clearly and as automatically as could Visitor and his dad. He did, however, have *a good itch*‡ to get back out on the streets and in the parks of Vienna to take spy photos which were of value to Visitor and the American Intelligence Group in Vienna. In sum, he wanted again to experience the fear and then the triumph that comes when he defeated the *genuine*§ evil knights of his day's world—the Russians—trying to capture Austria which had battled foreign armies for a thousand years. *Fittingly,*⁋ he would soon get his chance. Fortunately, he would not be on his own but instead he would have support and guidance.

On the Friday after Major Gorski went back to Warsaw, Visitor arranged to visit the Hale's castle in the evening. He wanted to discuss downtown Vienna and what David had accomplished so far in the parks within the First or International District at the very heart of historic Vienna. The photos David had taken were proving to be quite valuable to Visitor as he planned future intelligence operations against the Russians who had their Headquarters at Vienna's Imperial Hotel quite close to

---

*   Overwhelming: Massive, enormous.
†   To See the Big Picture: Understand the most important things happening in Austria and across Eastern Europe.
‡   A Good Itch: A very strong desire or hope.
§   Genuine: Real, not imagined.
⁋   Fittingly: For good reasons.

the Russian World War II Memorial and nearby *Stadtpark.** At 8:30 in the evening, Visitor arrived at the Hale castle through the garden after he came up the river by boat—Visitor was clearly determined to protect the operational security and cover of the Hales, even if it meant that getting to the castle for him was a bit damp, as well as *time consuming.*†

Dr. Matt Hale greeted Visitor and suggested they go to the kitchen and have their discussion over a cup of coffee and a slice of strudel that Katrina Vogel had baked in the afternoon. David was upstairs going through his growing collection of photographs and would join them later if Visitor thought that would be useful. Visitor said that would indeed be good because what the Intelligence Group was planning operationally very much concerned the boy. Regardless, Visitor wanted to first bounce off the doctor the operational plan and get his approval even before raising it with Hale's enthusiastic son. As the meeting began, Visitor explained to Matt Hale how the worsening security situation was *altering*‡ the Americans' plan to deal with the growing Soviet Russian threat.

To begin with, Washington was concerned that the Red Army was showing signs of strengthening their forces, possibly to be able to attack the Western Allies as soon as next Spring— maybe even sooner! The military leaders at the Pentagon had decided, therefore, to prepare their military forces in Germany

---

*   Stadtpark: People's park, in German. This is the largest park in the International Zone and quite handy for spies from the Russian Embassy headquarters in the Imperial Hotel. Because the Russians had reached Vienna first, they had chosen the most impressive hotel and occupied it until leaving Austria altogether in 1955.

†   Time Consuming: Slower than simply driving there by car.

‡   Altering: Changing.

and Austria for stay-behind operations that would help slow down and possibly stop the Soviet Red Army before it would be able to push through and conquer all of Western Europe. So, throughout the American Zones in both Germany and Austria, the U.S. Army had secretly started burying military weapons and war-fighting supplies to help defend these countries should the Soviets launch a surprise attack. At the very least, they would be able to slow the Red Army *advance** until the American and British forces in the U.S. and England were able to respond. Because the Soviets had so many *armored tanks*† as the *backbone*‡ of their military power, the Americans were hiding thousands of *bazookas*§ in caves and salt mines as well as burying them in fields throughout Central and Western Austria and Germany.

Visitor then spoke about the reason why he needed to see the Hales *on short notice*.¶ Visitor explained that the American Intelligence Group in Vienna had decided NOT to send the Hale-Castle Nazi Gold bars to the United States. Since the bars had most likely been made from gold the Nazis stole from the Austrians themselves, it would not be right for the U.S. to take it out of the country. Instead, the four gold bars would remain in Austria in case the Red Army invaded—the gold could then be used to buy weapons to help fight off the Communist forces. In fact, Visitor said, the gold bars would be buried in Vienna, probably within the International Zone. But

---

* Advance: Progress conquered territory.
† Armored tanks: War machines that have several inches of steel covering.
‡ Backbone: The strongest structure and foundation.
§ Bazookas: Weapons carried by soldiers that fire shells that can destroy a heavy armored steel tank.
¶ On Short Notice: So quickly.

where? Since the Hales had found the gold in the first place, the Intelligence Group wanted their input and suggestions on where to put the gold bars so they would not be *stumbled upon** accidentally.

Matt Hale, at this point, called David to join the men in the kitchen to see if he could think of a safe place for the gold bars. When David heard the call, he set aside his batch of photos and started down the back stairway in his usual acrobatic way. He entered the kitchen and was pleased to find Katrina's strudel and the hot chocolate his dad had prepared. He then got a big surprise that went beyond anything he might have dreamed—Visitor proceeded to ask him where he would bury the four 25 pound gold bars in downtown Vienna if he wanted them never to be found by anyone, accidentally. That's right— for years and years to come! After all, David had become as familiar with the city layout and design as had anyone in the American Intelligence Group. Being such a *precocious†* young boy, David just might come up with the best solution! At this point, David sat there eating his strudel, thought a while, and said he had two questions for Visitor: Should the gold be buried altogether in one location or separately in four—and must it be buried inside or outside?

Visitor was so glad he had the boy on his team because playing hide and seek was something more natural to kids than adults. But, in answer to his first question, Visitor said that each gold bar should be hidden away from and *independent of‡* the other three. "And, oh, outside, definitely outside!"

---

*   Stumbled Upon: Found by a stranger's plain luck.
†   Precocious: More alert and capable than most other eleven year olds.
‡   Independent of: Separate or away from.

After talking and speculating for nearly two hours, it was getting late, so Visitor suggested they *call it a night** and meet the following evening to come up with an effective plan that would *practically guarantee*† the gold would remain safe and available to the Austrian Army in case the Russians were to attack. Recently, the American Intelligence Group's own *assessment*‡ was that, because things were getting so bad across Eastern Europe, the chances of a Red Army attack in the next six months was somewhere around *fifty-fifty.*§

Before leaving, Visitor explained the method he would use to bury the gold—David needed this information so he would be able to do his part in the operation. The four gold bars, Visitor explained, had already been *re-cast*⁹ to remove the Nazi Swastika on each bar found in the Hale castle cellar. Instead, each new bar now had *imprinted*** the historic Austrian Black Eagle symbol and weighed almost 25 pounds. Visitor told David his job would be to find four hiding places in the parks of Vienna and mark each burial spot with the railroad spikes Visitor brought with him. Once David selected a site, the boy should use his foot to drive the spike into the ground so Visitor can find it with a magnet that would *assure*†† him he was burying the gold in precisely the right place. Each of the

---

*   Call It a Night: Decide to do no more that day.
†   Practically Guarantee: Make just about certain.
‡   Assessment: Judgment or conclusion.
§   Fifty-Fifty: Just about the same chance that an attack would take place or not (50% to 50%).
⁹   Re-Cast: Melted down and placed in new molds.
**   Imprinted: Printed by force or pressure and therefore a permanent marking deep within each gold bar.
††   Assure: Guarantee or make certain.

four hiding place reports should include a sketch, a photo and a written description of the site.

David then asked Visitor how he would bury the bars so no one else would notice that some recent digging had taken place. Visitor explained that one of his engineers had designed a tool that could drive a pipe deeply underground—the engineer had shown he was able to drill a *vertical hole** three-inches wide and just over 6 feet underground. This tool would be used to drill the hole, then each gold bar would be pushed down deep enough so that anyone doing gardening or planting bushes would not reach the level of the gold—at least six feet underground! Each *insertion*† of a gold bar, and filling the hole with dirt, would take the Visitor team about 20–30 minutes from start to finish.

After Visitor left their meeting by way of the river, father and son chatted for a while longer. David was delighted the gold bars were not being shipped back to Fort Knox in Kentucky where America's golf reserves are *safeguarded*‡ in the country's most heavily-protected fortress. With tons and tons of America's gold bars already buried at Fort Knox in huge underground vaults, the boy figured that 'Thor's gold,' as David called it, belonged and could be more useful right there in Austria. As the clock struck midnight, David headed up to his room. For almost an hour, he lay wide awake as he thought about the dozen or so parks he had visited, most of which were either in the American or International Zone. He then fell into a very deep sleep.

---

*   Vertical hole: Straight down towards the center of the earth.
†   Insertion: Burying or implanting.
‡   Safeguarded: Protected by heavy security.

When the sun came up and David awoke and—for reasons not clear to the junior spy—he thought he had his answer. To make sure the gold would not be discovered accidentally or by chance, he needed hiding places that would never change—not for years, not for decades, and not even for centuries. "The *memorials**" he said out loud, of course, "THE MEMORIALS!"

When the boy got out of bed this Saturday morning, he sat at his desk and began putting together a plan. Ordinarily, he would have started the day by going downstairs looking for his dad to tell him what he was thinking. But, this time, he decided he would, on his own, do some deep thinking and try coming up with a complete solution to 'the gold problem.' This time, he wanted to offer his dad and Visitor not *merely*† a general idea without *details*.‡ Instead, he would think through the entire problem the way his dad and Visitor seemed to do when faced with an important and difficult intelligence matter—they took their time—they made sure they *took everything into account*.§

Yes, this time, the plan David offered would be A to Z complete! To be certain he would be proposing a plan of action that was *accurate*,⁏ David decided to go into downtown Vienna for the day and check out the three parks he had in mind. He asked

---

*   The Memorials: Statues and monuments built in public parks and along public avenues in remembrance of former battles, victories, heroes and famous leaders and citizens.

†   Merely: Only or simply.

‡   Details: The many minor or less important things that go into a plan to build something or solve a problem. David remembered the checklist his father had put together and used when rescuing the Polish scientist in Linz.

§   Took Everything into Account: Made sure they covered all fine points needed for complete planning.

⁏   Accurate: Exactly right, correct.

his dad for a ride into the city so he and Thor could spend Saturday morning in the parks before they became too crowded with weekend family visitors. Before leaving the previous day, Visitor said he would probably do the burials of the four gold bars the next weekend, probably at 2:00 in the early morning of August 2nd when that night's full moon would give Visitor enough *luminescence** to see what he was doing. Once he found the railroad spikes David had *implanted,*† Visitor would drill the four holes a couple of yards down into the soil. Fortunately, Vienna's parks were closed at night so Visitor knew he could visit the three parks without being seen and plant the gold bars in total secrecy.

The parks David selected were within walking distance of each other, so he was sure he could scout them out on foot within 2 to 3 hours. He began at Vienna's City Park (called Stadtpark in German) that happened to be the largest public area in the International Zone of Central Vienna. Located near the center of the city, Stadtpark had two monuments that each had a dirt-grass area where a deep but narrow hole could be dug for *inserting*‡ a gold bar. David and Thor walked around Stadtpark for close to an hour and came across two statues that seemed just right for Visitor's purposes. Composer Franz Schubert's statue had been designed and built in 1872, some 75 years earlier than David's and Thor's *expedition*§ in late July 1947. The other statue in Stadtpark David assumed would never be moved was that of Johann Strauss, Jr. His monument showed

---

*   Luminescence: Brightness.
†   Implanted: Buried or placed.
‡   Inserting: Pushing a 2–3 inch gold bar into the ground.
§   Expedition: A trip for exploring.

Monument to Composer Franz Schubert, Vienna

Monument to Composer Johann Strauss, Vienna

the Waltz-King *composer** playing a violin and was coated in a gold-colored metal. It had been erected in 1921 and was possibly the most popular statue in all of Vienna.

The next park where David found a statue he liked for the project was in the People's Garden (Volksgarten in German) which is part of the Hofburg Palace in the center of Vienna. This *majestic*[†] monument had been built in 1875 in memory of Austria's favorite poet and writer, Franz Grillparzer.

The fourth and final memorial David selected was that of Franz Joseph Haydn who not only composed great music, but had been a *beloved*[‡] teacher of both Beethoven and Mozart. Haydn died in 1809 and, though his *remains*[§] had been later moved to another cemetery, the original gravestone stood in Haydnpark, named after him in downtown Vienna.

David and Thor were waiting at the entrance to Stadtpark when his dad drove up. The boy was not surprised to see that so many Viennese families had arrived at the park since much of the city was still recovering from the bombing and families needed to get away from their own badly-bombed homes and get some fresh air. Father and son returned to the castle and David set about writing the plan for his early-Sunday visit to the three parks to plant the four spikes that Visitor would need to put the gold bars where they belonged.

---

*   Composer: Writer of music.
†   Majestic: Spectacular or amazing.
‡   Beloved: Highly respected and
§   Remains: Bones.

Monument to Poet Franz Grillparzer, Vienna

Monument to Composer Joseph Hayden, Vienna

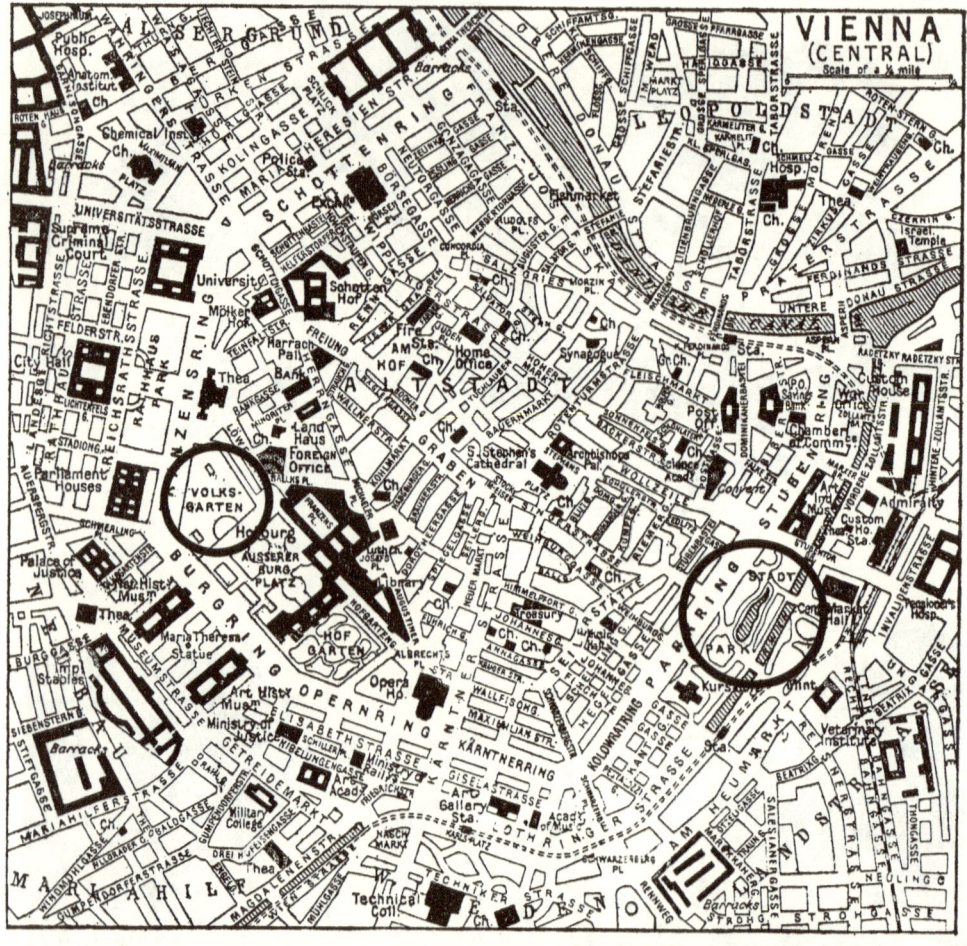

Map of downtown Vienna around the end of WWII, with circles showing
the locations of Volksgarten and Stadtpark. Haydnpark is off the map to
the southwest (near the lower left corner of this page).

12

American Baseball Comes to Vienna

By mid-point in the summer of '47—while Europe and Asia were in growing *turmoil** from the Communist armies of both the Russians and the Chinese—Americans in the States were enjoying their lives as though the end of World War II meant the end also to serious foreign dangers. Families were moving on with their peacetime lives—buying homes and cars, going out to parks, picnics and beaches while baseball continued to be America's favorite sport. The New York Yankees continued in their *dominance*† of the game which began back in 1919 when the Boston Red Sox sold baseball homerun great, Babe Ruth, to the New York Yankees. In 1947, to be precise, the Yankees would win 40 more games than they lost while the Red Sox would end up far behind, in third place, trailing behind both the Yankees and the Detroit Tigers.

So what does Major League baseball in 1947 have to do with the Cold War in Eastern Europe and a boy named David? Well, at the time when Americans were living their lives with a high degree of *normalcy*,‡ the junior spy set aside his baseball concerns and was engaged in the growing battle of America against Soviet Russia. And by the last week of July 1947—some 2,000

---

* Turmoil: Chaos and troubles.
† Dominance: Winning ways in the competition.
‡ Normalcy: The ordinary way things are done when there is not a war or total chaos.

miles to the east of New York and Boston in Vienna—lifelong baseball fan David Hale was preparing a plan to bury gold bars to do battle, not for a baseball trophy or great publicity, but for the quiet satisfaction that comes when freedom itself wins against *tyranny*.*

Accordingly,† when the boy got thinking about the parks, he decided to connect his Vienna monuments plan to American baseball in a way that would protect the operation's security in the years ahead—he would create and use a code that would be *unbreakable*‡ and *enduring*.§ In fact, even the great Russian chess players, he thought, would not be able to unscramble David's code. It would be powerful and operationally secure. David felt *confident*⁋ it would meet with Visitor's approval.

Before starting to write up his plan, he reviewed the baseball book he had bought in Cooperstown, New York at the National Baseball Hall of Fame. David examined the records of four players who were voted into The Hall in its first two years, back in 1936 and 1937. He chose, from the 1936 group, Ty Cobb and Babe Ruth. From the 1937 group he chose great pitcher Cy Young and great batter Napoleon or 'Nap' LaJoie. In each case, David based his selection on career records that, even ten years later in 1947, were considered long-lasting and probably unbreakable.

Detroit Tigers batter Ty Cobb's Lifetime Batting Average was .366. To come up with a measurement that made sense

---

*   Tyranny: The harsh rule by a cruel leader or group over the lives of simple citizens.
†   Accordingly: Therefore, or as a result.
‡   Unbreakable: A secret code not able to be understood or unraveled.
§   Enduring: Lasts forever, not temporary.
⁋   Confident: Sure of himself

and would help Visitor find the railroad spikes in the middle of the night, David decided he would take Cobb's 366 as centimeters—then he would make the 366 a simpler measurement by *converting** it to feet. How would he do that? He remembered his dad's math class where he learned to convert centimeters to feet by dividing the number of centimeters by 30.48. THE FIRST SPIKE IN VOLKSGARTEN PARK WOULD BE PLACED 12 FEET EAST OF THE FRANZ GRILLPARZER MONUMENT. (366 divided by 30.48 equals 12 feet.) Using the centimeters-to-feet conversion method, David did the same conversion to the Hall of Fame career number of the other three American ballplayers.

New York Yankee slugger Babe Ruth, for example, had 714 Career Home Runs. So, David divided Ruth's 714 home runs by 30.48 which meant that THE SECOND SPIKE WOULD BE PLANTED 23.4 FEET FROM THE FRANZ JOSEPH HAYDN MONUMENT IN HAYDN PARK. (714 divided by 30.48 equals 23.4 feet.)

Cleveland pitching great Cy Young had 511 Career Winning Games. THE THIRD SPIKE WOULD BE PLANTED 16.8 FEET FROM THE FRANZ SCHUBERT MONUMENT IN STADTPARK. (511 divided by 30.48 equals 16.8 feet.)

Finally, Nap LaJoie had baseball's Single-Year Highest Batting Average of .426. THE FOURTH SPIKE, then, WOULD BE PLANTED 14 FEET FROM THE JOHANN STRAUSS MONUMENT, ALSO IN STADTPARK. (426 divided by 30.48 equals 14 feet.)

---

*   Converting: In Math, one must divide by a conversion factor that is correct. For example, to change feet to inches, one uses a conversion factor of 12 inches being equal to one feet. So, when David needed to change the large centimeter numbers of the four Hall of Fame players to feet, he divided each player's Hall of Fame record number by the correct conversion number—30.48. As a result, Visitor would have a small and simple measurement to find the buried spikes. After all, he would be doing the burying of the gold at night.

In all four cases, a gold bar would be buried directly *due east** of the front left corner of each monument exactly at the distance shown for that particular player and monument. Needless to say, the secret code itself would be explained on an entirely separate paper. The Austrian parks and monuments in David's report to the American Intelligence Group would be re-named "The Ty Cobb," the second would be "The Babe Ruth," the third would be called "The Cy Young," and the last one would be known as "The Nap LaJoie."

To locate the spike he would use in burying the gold, Visitor would be using an American tape measure in feet and inches. He would also be using a *compass†* to find the spikes and be burying the gold bars exactly to the east of each monument. The boy then took a clothesline and cut it to give himself lengths of ropes of 12 feet, 23.4 feet, 16.8 feet and 14 feet that he would use with Thor's help to bury—and Visitor would later use to locate—the railroad spikes that would tell him where each gold bar should be hidden.

On Saturday night, Visitor was back at the castle to review the plan David had been working on and make certain that everyone—Matt Hale, David and Visitor himself—understood how David was going to bury the spikes and how Visitor would later be burying the gold bars.

Needless to say, when David explained his coded system to his dad and to Visitor, each of the men was exceedingly pleased

---

*   Due east: Exactly to the east.

†   Compass: A hand-held instrument with a magnetized needle that points to the North Pole and permits its user to locate North and South, East and West. In this case, David chose to have each gold bar buried east of each monument's front-left base.

that the boy had put so much thought into it. Visitor was especially impressed by the boy's deep interest in operational security. But Visitor wanted to know why David had *devised**
a coded system in the first place. After all, the only people who would know anything about the secret gold burial in Vienna would be the Hales and members of Vienna's American Intelligence Group.

The boy explained that in an earlier meeting Visitor had mentioned that the four gold bars were worth around $70,000—in 1947, that was a *great deal of money*.† So, David reasoned, why not try to make certain that no one in the future is tempted to steal the gold bars. After all, they were being hidden to protect Austria and certainly not to enrich a thief—whether Russian, Austrian or American! Visitor and Matt Hale both agreed that the junior spy was correct and his security warning would be followed. Visitor then remarked: "Not everyone is a *saint*,‡ so I agree with you that we must be extra careful. I will make absolutely sure that the secrecy of the 'David Code' and 'Thor's Gold Bars' are protected long into the future—in fact, longer than Russia presents a danger to other nations and people. Knowing the Russians as I do, I imagine that may well turn out to be a very long time."

Visitor left and both Hales went to bed.

---

* Devised: Created.

† Great Deal of Money: By 2023, for example, four gold bars weighing 100 pounds would today be worth Two Million, Eight Hundred Thousand Dollars! (100 pounds = 1600 ounces at $1,750 per ounce = $2,800,000.)

‡ Saint: An honest person who does everything right and would never steal, even a fortune in gold.

On Sunday morning at *sunrise**—5:22 am—father and son headed for downtown Vienna with Thor, as usual, sticking his handsome head out through the Mercedes rear window. They went first to Stadtpark with its Strauss and Schubert monuments, then on to Volksgarten and finally to Haydnpark. David brought along his carrying sack with the four railroad spikes, the four lengths of rope as well as the U.S. Army compass that Visitor had given him the previous week. Around his neck he hung the Leica camera so he looked like a bird watcher out for an early Sunday walk.

When he arrived at the Schubert statue, he took out the 16.8 foot rope and got Thor to hold it in his mouth just above the front left corner of the monument's foundation. David then took the compass and, after watching the needle point to the North, he was able to find the Easterly direction. He then placed one of the spikes on the ground while Thor just stood there seeming to enjoy his part in whatever game David was now playing. At this point, the boy dropped his end of the rope, looked all around to be sure that no one in the area was watching, and then drove the spike down into the soil with his boot. He then covered it with a handful of dirt.

And so it went with the three parks, the four monuments, the four spikes and the four lengths of rope. David also took several photos of each park and monument. The average time spent at each site turned out to be less than fifteen minutes. The entire time spent in downtown Vienna was a little less than two hours. David had some work to do writing his report, developing

---

*   Sunrise: When the sun in the early morning comes over the horizon and gradually brightens the world.

the film as well as drawing his sketches. His dad had a busy morning writing reports on the week's hospital visits. Dr. Hale happened to have a medical meeting scheduled at mid-week in downtown Vienna—he was able to pass David's *casing report** along to Visitor, who planned to bury the golden treasure in the Austrian capital on August's first full-moon night. The burial *phase*† of the operation went smoothly and Visitor was able to get it done with the help of the Intelligence Group's *technical wizard*‡ who had invented and built the *excavation*§ tool.

When Visitor sent a message to the Hales that he had buried the gold bars without difficulty—and especially to thank David—the junior spy sat on the castle wall and reviewed in his mind the previous week's activity. He thought back to the rainy day Thor and he had found the Nazi trunks in the castle north tunnel. He recalled the excitement he felt when he first showed his dad the entire cache of gold, money and documents on Germany's top 100 war criminals. And then he *mulled over*¶ in his mind how the four precious gold bars now lay buried in Vienna's parks when, instead, they could have been caught up in the *Nazi South American ratline.*** "What a different outcome," he thought. "What a great way to be spending my

---

*   Casing Report: A report that shows the locations where spy material is buried—in this case, the four spikes.

†   Phase: Part.

‡   Technical wizard: One so gifted in working in engineering/ technical things that he seems to be almost a magician.

§   Excavation: Hole digging for building a home, a highway or—as in this case—burying gold bars.

¶   Mulled over: Pondered or was thinking things over.

**   Nazi South American Ratline: This was the organized secret operation after WWII to help Nazi war criminals escape Germany and Austria and avoid being punished for the war crimes they had committed during the war.

summer! What a wonderful dog is Thor! Oh my, I wonder—as in Hollywood movies—whether this might be The End."

Visitor and Major Gorski Review Warsaw Map
to Plan Future Clandestine Meetings

Epilogue
The Vienna Trilogy

Escape to the West – Book I
Nazis on the Run – Book II
Stopping the Russian Bear – Book III

The summer of 1947 for junior spy David Hale came to an end, much as the boy feared, without anything spectacular happening in the spy world beyond what had already occurred. The Polish scientist, Dr. Kaminsky, was working in the United States on nuclear safety. The four gold bars were resting peacefully near monuments in three of downtown Vienna's parks. The trio of former Gestapo Nazis were entirely out of the way; in fact, KAPUT! The recruited intelligence and trained spy was back in Poland where he would be supported by Visitor who was transferred to Warsaw in the middle of August. So, the Hale boy, in the course of a single summer, had assembled both great memories and satisfaction that his remaining in Vienna had been worthwhile.

Dr. Matt Hale and David did travel back to the States in late August and joined mother and daughter for two weeks of swimming, fishing, hiking and family conversation. Not discussed were the operational capers that had been the focus of Matt and David's summer. They were, after all, security-classified matters that would be shared only on a need-to-know basis. Mother and Ellie did notice a couple of things about David that caught their attention. To begin with, his German skills had improved greatly over what was the case back in June. The other change that Mom and sister Ellie saw in David was that he seemed more grown up and had become more responsible and serious.

Part of the reason they did not dwell on these changes in David is that they were told that Dr. Hale had been given an offer to take charge of the Refugee and Displaced Persons Medical programs in Germany as well as Austria. The good news for the family was that the Hales took a vote and everyone agreed they should keep the castle. David seemed to perk up when he heard he might get to visit Berlin with his dad in the fall. "Lots of spies in Berlin, Dad?"

"Yes, Son. Lots and lots."